THE RAINBOW SERPENT

A KULIPARI NOVEL

BY **TREVOR PRYCE** WITH **JOEL NAFTALI**

ILLUSTRATED BY **SANFORD GREENE**

AMULET BOOKS
NEW YORK

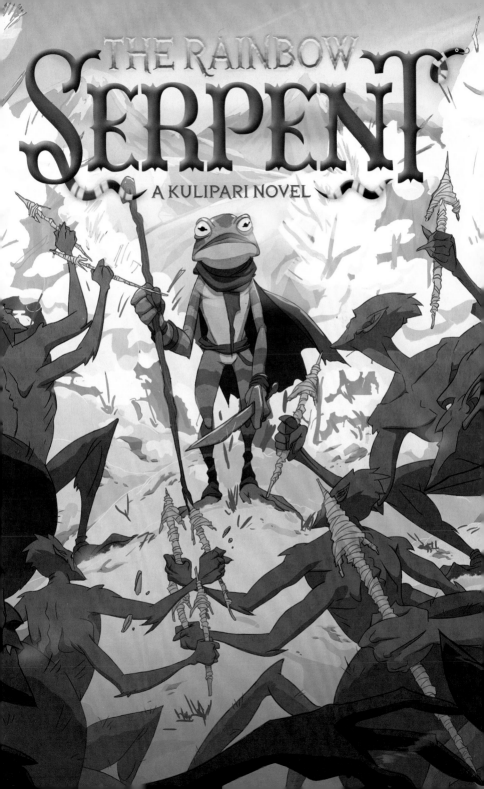

THE RAINBOW
SERPENT

A KULIPARI NOVEL

Library of Congress Cataloging-in-Publication Data

Pryce, Trevor.
The Rainbow Serpent : a Kulipari novel / by Trevor Pryce ;
with Joel Naftali ; illustrated by Sanford Greene.
pages cm
Summary: The frog warriors search for their dreamcasting
turtle friend, Yabber, who insists he knows who holds the key
to saving the Amphibilands: the Rainbow Serpent, an ancient
god who brought life to the Australian outback.
ISBN 978-1-4197-1309-5 (hardback)
[1. Frogs—Fiction. 2. Animals—Fiction.
3. Magic—Fiction. 4. Fantasy—Fiction.]
I. Naftali, Joel. II. Greene, Sanford, illustrator. III. Title.
PZ7.P9493496Rai 2014
[Fic]—dc23
2014009732

Text copyright © 2014 Trevor Pryce
Illustrations copyright © 2014 Sanford Greene
Book design by Sara Corbett and Kate Fitch

Printed and bound in China
10 9 8 7 6 5 4 3 2 1

Amulet Books are available at special discounts
when purchased in quantity for premiums and promotions
as well as fundraising or educational use. Special editions
can also be created to specification. For details, contact
specialsales@abramsbooks.com or the address below.

ABRAMS
THE ART OF BOOKS SINCE 1949
115 West 18th Street
New York, NY 10011
www.abramsbooks.com

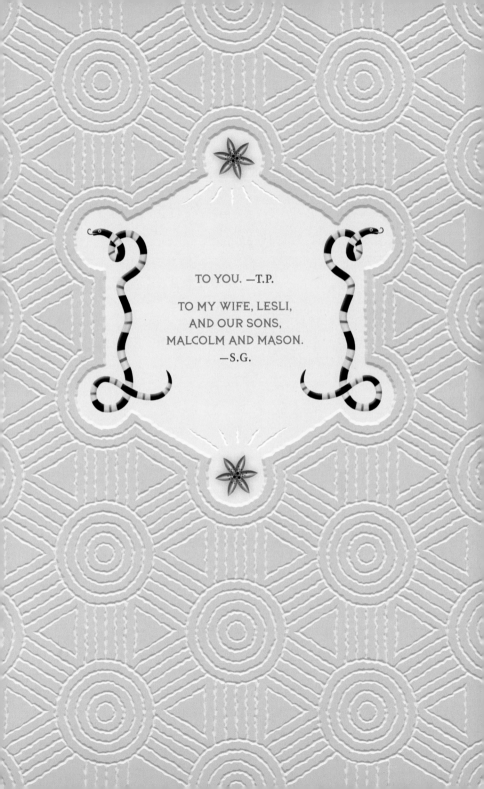

TO YOU. —T.P.

TO MY WIFE, LESLI,
AND OUR SONS,
MALCOLM AND MASON.
—S.G.

STARGAZER'S
BURROW

PPI'S
RROW

ATYPUS VILLAGE

BAT CAVE

THE OUTBACK

SNOWY MOUNTAINS

TARGANGIL

YARRANGOBILLY
CAVES

MAP OF THE
PLATYPUS VILLAGE
AND SURROUNDINGS

DAREL

GURNUGAN (GEE)
DAREL'S BEST FRIEND

GEE'S MOTHER AND FATHER

DAREL'S MOTHER
A WOOD FROG

ARABANOO
A TREE FROG

THUMA

THARTA

DAREL'S YOUNGER TRIPLET SIBLINGS

COORAH

COORAH'S FATHER

A HEALER

TIPI

ARABANOO'S GANG

DAREL'S FRIEND AND AN APPRENTICE HEALER

FROGS AND PLATYPUSES

LORD MARMOO
LEADER OF THE SCORPIONS

COMMANDER PIGO

LORD MARMOO'S SECOND-IN-COMMAND

TAIPAN SNAKES

OLD JIR
A FORMER KULIPARI

QUOBA
A KULIPARI SCOUT

BURNU
THE KULIPARI LEADER

CHIEF OLBA
LEADER OF THE FROGS

DINGO
A KULIPARI

PONTO
THE KULIPARI HEALER

YABBER

A TURTLE AND
DREAMCASTER

STARGAZER

PIPPI

A YOUNG PLATYPUS

LEADER OF
THE PLATYPUSES

PIRRI

PIRRI'S
SISTER

VERSUS

SCORPIONS AND SPIDERS

BLUE BAND
BEES

QUEEN JARRAH'S
HANDMAIDENS

QUEEN JARRAH
RULER OF THE SPIDERS

ARK CLOUDS GATHERED OVER THE hills of the outback, and a dry wind blew. A thousand spiderwebs shimmered at the mouth of a rocky cave.

Inside the cave, dozens of pale forms dangled from the ceiling. When the breeze touched them, they twisted and stretched . . . then dropped from the craggy roof. Spreading their wings, they took flight: a swarm of ghost bats, with huge ears and white bellies and teeth sharp enough to kill.

They poured from the cave in a swirling cloud, swooping past the glowing spiderwebs.

"It's the spider queen," a scowling bat said in a whispery voice. *"She commands us to hunt."*

A red-eyed bat hissed. *"Queen Jarrah is an eight-legged guano-head."*

"She does only what Lord Marmoo tells her. The scorpion lord is the real power."

"No, no," the red-eyed bat whispered. "It is the queen who is in charge now. And she'll kill anyone who stands against her. Like the wallaby troop—she dried up their springs with her nightcasting."

"They died . . . of thirst?" the scowling bat asked with a nervous shiver.

The other bat nodded. "*Jarrah's power comes from dust and dryness. Now that the turtle king is dead, she'll turn the whole outback into a desert, fit only for spiders and scorps.*"

"*But she'll let us have water?*"

"*Enough to survive—if we obey.*"

With a tremor of fear, they joined the pale cloud of bats flitting through the evening, following the hill downward toward the swamp.

Looking for prey.

Deep in her snug burrow, Okipippi woke early—which for a platypus meant "before sunset"—and yawned and stretched her tail. She drowsed in her comfy twig nest for a few minutes, listening to her parents snoring away in the other room.

Then she rubbed her eyes and noticed that her sister's nest was empty. Pirra was probably already on the river, floating around with her friends. Pippi wasn't old enough to swim in the river before dark, but that didn't bother her. She liked to spend most of her time with the Stargazer anyway.

The platypus tribe didn't have a chief or a king or a queen. If they needed advice, they went to the Stargazer, an old gray-furred platypus with notched ears and bright eyes. She taught the newborn pups after they hatched in the deep, mud-walled nurseries, and she had her own kind of magic. Not dreamcasting, like the turtles. Not nightcasting, like the spiders. The Stargazer simply twirled herself into a trance, then focused on the distant whispering of the Rainbow Serpent, the ancient god who'd brought life to the Australian outback.

Pippi loved the legends of the Rainbow Serpent.

She liked the one about the colors of the Serpent dripping onto the Kulipari to give them power, and the one about her great-great-grandparents digging endless burrows beneath the outback—tunnels that connected the deep waters of the Amphibilands to the rest of the land.

But her favorite story explained how the Serpent had created the platypuses in its own image. Just as a rainbow contained many different colors, a platypus contained many different parts: a duck-like bill; webbed feet; thick, waterproof fur; and a chunky tail. The males even had a poison spur on one ankle!

Maybe that's why the platypuses followed the Serpent more closely than anyone else. At least, the Stargazer did. She didn't actually *talk* to the Rainbow Serpent, but she deciphered messages in the ripples and splashes of the river's current. There were a hundred myths and tales and legends about the Serpent, but they all agreed that the ancient water god had breathed life into a dry land, creating streams and lakes and pools.

After one final yawn, Pippi wandered into the kitchen, grabbed a crayfish tail, and called, "Mom! Dad! I'm going outside!"

"Don't go too far," came her father's sleepy voice. "You're still a platypup."

"Okay!" she called back, as she headed for the burrow entrance.

Old trees rose along the wide river that snaked through the platypus village, and their roots twined down along the riverbank—some gnarled and thick, others as skinny as kite strings. Most of the burrows were hidden behind the curtain of roots, dozens of neat holes just above the waterline.

Using her wide webbed foot, Pippi pushed aside the dangling roots. She looked at the blue water shifting to gray in the fading light of day. Furry brown platypuses floated lazily in the river, getting ready to hunt, their duck-bills breaking the surface and their beaver-like tails swishing behind them.

Pippi spotted her sister. But since Pippi was too young to slip into the water until the safety of nightfall, she stayed where she was and ate the last bite of crayfish tail. Then she climbed the riverbank, walking on her knuckles to protect the sensitive webbing between her toes. Most platypuses didn't like walking on dry land, but Pippi didn't mind. Pirra called her a weirdo and their parents called her a dreamer, but the Stargazer just said that she was curious.

She headed upstream, toward the gentle roar of the rapids. Mist drifted through the air, and she paused now and then to lick the moisture from her fur. Walking on dry land made her thirsty.

Finally, she stopped beneath a riberry tree that grew from the bank of the river. Roots dangled over a wide burrow mouth, and she parted them with her bill.

"Stargazer?" she called. "Are you awake?"

"Hmm . . . I *think* so," the Stargazer's soft voice said from within. "But what if I'm asleep and dreaming that I'm awake?"

Pippi giggled. "Then you wouldn't be talking to me!"

"Come in, Pippi," the Stargazer said with a laugh. "I'm in the dripping room."

Pippi waddled deeper into a comfy curving tunnel that ballooned here and there into a kitchen, living room, and bedrooms. It looked like everyone else's burrow, except the Stargazer also had a "dripping room"—a candlelit earthen chamber with one wall of solid rock. Water trickled down the wall, making damp, crisscrossing tracks and splatters.

Pippi found the Stargazer staring at the wall. The elderly platypus's small eyes were bright in the flickering light.

"I feel the call of the Rainbow Serpent," the Stargazer told her. "An important message, but I can't quite make it out."

Pippi settled beside her and squinted at the wall.

"What do you see?" the Stargazer asked.

"Mostly rock," Pippi answered. "And some water."

The Stargazer *tsk*ed. "Look closer. The Rainbow Serpent speaks to us through water."

Pippi wrinkled her bill and peered intently at the wall.

Water dripped. Patches of moisture caught the glint of the candles. The roar of the rapids outside sounded like a thousand platypuses murmuring. The damp tracks of the water seemed almost to form a picture, a mural, a—

The Stargazer gasped. "There! Did you see?"

"What? Where?" Pippi blinked. *Had* she seen something? "I'm not sure."

"I'm afraid . . ." The Stargazer stepped closer to the wall, and for a long moment just studied the dripping water. Then she rubbed her face and sighed. "I'm afraid it's bad news, Pippi—indeed, the worst I've seen."

Pippi shifted nervously. "What's wrong?"

"We're in danger, the whole tribe."

"F-f-from what?"

"I think . . . birds? It's not clear. But something in the air."

"When—now? I'll run and tell everyone!"

"Wait. It's not just us. The whole outback is under threat—all the wet places, all the streams and springs." The Stargazer swayed as her eyes became unfocused. "A war is coming . . . a battle for water. The final battle. The scorpions and spiders and—"

"*They* can't hurt us!" Pippi said, her voice squeaking. "Everyone knows bugs can't swim. We'll hide in the river if they come."

"But the spider queen knows that we listen to the Rainbow Serpent, and she knows the Serpent will oppose her. She'll try to kill us, to silence the Serpent—nobody else heeds the signs the way we do. I see villages burned, Pippi. Death and destruction and wetlands turned into desert . . ."

Pippi's bill trembled in fear. "Wh-wh-what should I do?"

"We need help. We need the Blue Sky King."

"The what?"

"The frog called Darel," the Stargazer told her. "From the Amphibilands."

"Th-th-the one who beat the scorpion lord?"

The Stargazer nodded. "He is the key."

"Blue Sky King?" Pippi blinked in confusion. "Isn't he more of a Brown Pond Prince?"

The Stargazer smiled but didn't explain. Instead, she fell into a trance, humming to herself and shuffling from side to side as she gazed at the droplets of water on the rock wall.

"Stargazer?" Pippi said. But the old platypus was already lost in her dreaming.

Pippi knew better than to disturb her. With her heart pounding, she raced toward home. A war for water? The final war? Entire villages destroyed? A *frog*?

When she reached the village, she paused on a mossy log above the river to catch her breath. She spotted Pirra lazing in the current, but before Pippi could call out, a look of concern crossed her sister's face.

Turning to a friend floating nearby, Pirra asked, "What's that? Do you feel that?"

"Is it a shrimp?" her friend said, shaking his head slowly. Platypuses had a special sense beyond sight and smell and hearing—when they moved their bills back and forth, they could pick up electric fields created by other animals. "Water worms? I'm not feeling a tingle."

"I can't tell," Pirra said. "It's almost like it's coming from above."

Pippi spun to peer through the dusk, her fear suddenly as sharp as a blade.

"Water worms can't fly," the friend cracked. "You're getting as weird as your sister."

"Okipippi isn't weird!" Pirra could call Pippi that, but no one else could. "She's just . . . little."

Pippi almost smiled, happy that her sister had defended her, even if she had called her "little." Then she spotted motion in the trees: a flurry of white wings swooping and darting silently toward the river.

What *was* that? Not birds. Not fireflies. Then she realized, staring in shock. Bats! *Ghost bats!* She knew that the village sometimes fought the bats, if two hunting parties stumbled into each other in the middle of the night. But not like this—not an entire war party attacking the village for no reason.

"Bats!" Pippi screamed. "Bats are coming!"

Pirra swiveled in the water, finally seeing her. "Quiet, Pippi! You're going to wake the—"

"Ghost bats!" Pippi yelled, pointing frantically into the woods. "They're coming!"

"And now," the friend said with a snort, "she believes in ghosts. She's such a—" He stopped when the bats emerged from the trees, then screamed. "Bats! Help! Bats!"

As other young platypuses started yelling, the grown-ups sleepily emerged from the root-hidden burrows along the riverbank. They grumbled at the noise, then saw the bats angling directly toward them.

"Watch out!" Pippi cried. "Go back!"

It was too late. The ghost bats, their needle-sharp fangs bared, streamed through the air toward the slower-moving platypuses. A chubby platypus swiped at one with the poison spur on his back foot, but the bat simply flitted backward, higher in the air. A moment later, a gang of bats attacked the chubby platypus, teeth slashing. Pippi looked away in horror.

"Quick—get inside!" Pirra yelled. "Everyone, block off your burrows! Pippi, c'mon!"

Pippi started to slide down the muddy bank to the safety of the water, but three white bats, fangs glistening, suddenly appeared in front of her.

2

WITH A SQUEAL OF TERROR, Pippi shot sideways and clambered over a slippery rock, her claws scratching and sliding. One of the bats sank its teeth into her tail, and she shrieked at the stab of pain.

She spun in circles until she dislodged the bat, then fled through the underbrush. Shrubs and roots and fallen leaves blurred past. She raced on her aching knuckles, her mind blank with panic, as the shouts behind her grew fainter.

She ran and ran until finally she collapsed at the base of a tree fern, panting and exhausted. She licked at the bat bite, relieved to find she still had a tail. As the ache faded, she looked up and realized she didn't know where she was. And had no idea how to get home.

"Okay, don't panic," she muttered to herself. "*Think*. What would the Stargazer say? What would she tell me to do?"

She'd tell Pippi to find her way home. Or would she? She'd said that only one animal could help the tribe, and she'd been right about the attack from the air, so she must be right about the frog, too.

Pippi shivered under the tree fern. She *wanted* to find her way home, to check on her parents and sister and friends. But she *needed* to find Darel the frog before it was too late. Except she wasn't even sure where the Amphibilands was. Near the coast, she thought, but the coast was *big*.

She could follow the river, and hope it didn't lead her into dangerous marshland . . . or empty into a hole in the ground. Except she'd lost the river.

She glanced at the sky, wishing she could go into a trance and try to read the Rainbow Serpent's signs in the clouds, like the Stargazer sometimes did. But she couldn't, so she'd just have to decide for herself: Should she try to return home or search for the frog?

She closed her eyes and remembered the rivulets on the rock wall in the Stargazer's burrow. She imagined that each one was a raindrop, collecting in lakes that flowed into rivers that spread through the land, bringing color and lushness and life. She imagined what would happen if the spiders and scorps won the battle for water. She imagined rivers drying up and lakes turning into desert.

Then she rubbed her bill and sighed. She needed to find Darel the frog in the Amphibilands. She peeked around the tree fern. She didn't see any white bats flashing among the branches, so she headed off in the rising moonlight.

Toward the coast, toward—she hoped—the Amphibilands.

Toward help.

Pippi marched for hours as the stars twinkled in the sky. She froze perfectly still whenever a forest sound frightened her. Which was about every ten steps. She'd never traveled this far from the river's comforting gurgle or the safety of her burrow. She missed her parents and her sister, and she was starting to get hungry. There was no time to stop for food, though.

So she continued onward through the night, trying to pretend this was just one of the Stargazer's tales.

At the first faint light of dawn, her courage was rewarded—she smelled the sea in the air, a hint of brine and salt. She gave a happy thwack of her aching tail and decided to stop for a moment and have a snack.

She stuck her bill into the mud and wiggled it back and forth until she felt the tingle of little crawly tasty things. After gobbling down a few worms—crunchier than normal, and with way too many legs—she set off again.

She'd only gone a few hundred feet on her bruised knuckles when she heard a strange scuttling sound from the other side of a rocky gully. A sort of clicking *clitter-clatter*.

She stopped moving and peered into the shadows. She didn't see anything, but her bill told her there was something out there. Maybe more than *one* something.

Then a harsh voice slithered through the stillness. "Lord Marmoo promised us we'd be eating frog legs for breakfast, lunch, and dinner. But instead we're skulking in the forest. I miss the desert."

"Well," another voice said, "instead of frogs in our belly, Marmoo got a dagger in his."

Rasping laughter sounded, so cold and unfriendly that Pippi almost whimpered. Holding her breath, she hid beside a fallen branch, afraid to move. She heard an ugly sort of chewing, and then she saw them: two scorpion warriors, with segmented poison stingers swaying over their black carapaces. They were feeding on pincerfuls of snails. Blood smeared their mouthparts as they chewed and chattered, and Pippi trembled.

"I need something in *my* belly," the first scorpion grumbled. "I'm hungry."

"Yeah." The second scorpion spat out a bit of shell. "We need to kill something warm and fleshy soon."

Pippi gave a soft yelp of fear. *She* was warm and fleshy.

"Did you hear that?" The clattering of scorpion legs sounded again across the gully. "Something's near that dead branch."

"Yeah," the second one said. "I can smell it now . . . it'll be dead soon, too."

The clitter-clatter came closer, and Pippi panicked.

She heaved herself to her feet, scrambled over the fallen branch, and raced away. Leaves crunched and twigs whipped her face as she ran. Prickles snagged her thick coat as she stumbled through thorny bushes. She heard the scorpions draw closer as she slipped in a muddy puddle, raising a cloud of gnats.

For a long moment, she heard nothing but her own ragged breath . . . then the mocking voices of the scorpions sounded right behind her.

"Look at it try to run," one scorpion scoffed.

"Chubby water rat," the other said, ten feet behind Pippi. "It does look succulent."

Pippi wasn't sure what "succulent" meant, and she didn't want to find out.

She took off as fast as her stubby legs could go, but she was built for swimming, not for sprinting.

Her knuckles were aching, and her wide bill slowed her down. Only her fear kept her moving. She dashed across a grassy clearing and almost smacked into a tree but swerved at the last second, then tumbled down a shrubby hill, flipping and flopping, tail over bill.

She crashed to the ground at the bottom, dazed and breathless.

A second later, the scorpions skittered up. One of them prodded her with a pincer. "What is it?"

"I don't know," the other one said. "But it looks tasty."

"I—I—I'm not!" squeaked Pippi. "I'm very poisonous!"

"Not as poisonous as us," the first scorpion said. He raised his stinger, ready to strike.

3

PIPPI WISHED SHE HAD A STINGER of her own. Platypuses were the only *furry* creatures with poison stingers, but only platypus boys had them, which hardly seemed fair. Still, she had a little nonpoisonous spur on her leg, and she was so scared that she swiped at the scorps with it.

They laughed and swatted away her leg. Then one of them whipped its evil-looking stinger toward her belly.

"*Eep!*" Pippi yelped.

At that moment, a pod whizzed through the air and splattered against the scorpion's side.

Just inches from Pippi, the stinging tail swerved away. Purple juice oozed down the scorpion's segmented leg, and the scorpion spun toward whoever had thrown the pod.

Panting with terror, Pippi peeked past the scorps and saw a pretty frog with copper skin standing on a boulder, holding a slingshot.

"I made that goop from pepperbush," the frog explained to the scorpions. "It's spicy enough to burn right through your carapace."

The scorpions took a frightened step backward; then the one dripping with pepperbush goop stopped suddenly. His pincers snapped a few times, and he almost seemed to smile. "Sorry to disappoint you, frog girl," he said. "It doesn't burn at all."

"Not even a little?" the other scorpion asked.

"Yeah?" the frog asked. "Not even a little?"

"It's warm and prickly. And . . . " The first scorpion touched the goop with his pincer, then tasted the pepperbush juice. "And tasty."

"So we'll *finally* eat some frog legs," the second scorpion said, skittering toward the pretty frog. "In a nice pepper sauce."

"Oh, kookaburra!" the frog swore, looking more peeved than scared. "It's *still* not strong enough."

As the two scorpions swarmed up the boulder toward Pippi, a brown blur shot down at them from a tree branch. A brawny frog with yellow eyes swung his staff into the first scorpion's head, then leaped over the other scorpion's snapping pincer and lashed out with his powerful legs. The second scorpion went flying, bounced off the boulder, hurtled to the ground near Pippi, and lay there moaning.

The first scorpion shook his head and circled the brawny frog, his tail swaying, ready to strike.

"So you ran from Marmoo's army after he fell?" the frog asked. "We've been watching for stragglers like you."

The scorpion narrowed his side eyes. "What are frogs doing outside the Veil?"

"Get used to it," the frog said. "We're not scared anymore."

"You should be," the scorpion said, snapping with his pincer.

The brawny frog dodged, and the pretty frog with

the slingshot hopped closer to Pippi. She seemed gentle, but Pippi was so nervous that she curled into a defensive ball anyway.

"You're pathetic," the brawny frog told the scorpion. "I've seen polliwogs with scarier tails. I've seen tadpoles with—"

The scorpion lunged at the frog . . . and a bunch of long pink tongues shot from the branches overhead and caught the scorpion in a sort of web. The scorpion struggled to free himself, but before he could, the brawny frog whacked him on the head and knocked him unconscious.

The frog grinned as a handful of white-lipped frogs hopped down from the trees, making faces like they'd tasted something gross.

"Oh!" Pippi eyed the pretty frog nervously. "Th-th-thanks?"

"You're safe now," the frog told her, kneeling beside her. "We're not going to hurt you."

Hopping closer, the brawny frog grinned. "We don't even know what you *are*."

"Of *course* I know what she is," the girl frog said. "She's—"

"Don't tell me, Coorah!" the boy frog interrupted. "Let me guess. She looks like a cross between a possum and a pelican. Is she a possican? A pelicum?"

"I'm a platypus!" Pippi said, uncurling herself.

"Are you sure?" the frog said. "I still think you're a pelicossum."

"Of course I'm sure. I—" Pippi caught the mischievous expression on the frog's face. "Hey! You knew I was a platypus all along."

"Well . . . maybe," he admitted with a smile.

She smiled, too. He was just teasing her so she wouldn't be afraid.

"Though I thought you were called platy*pups* when you were young," he continued.

"Sure," she said. "Like you're frogpoles."

"Or pollifrogs," he said.

She giggled as the pretty frog named Coorah pulled something from her pouch.

"Here," Coorah said. "Let me put some salve on your cuts."

She rubbed a soothing cream on Pippi's tail. Her chilly froggy toe pads felt weird but also kind of nice.

"Thanks," Pippi said. "My name is Okipippi, but everyone calls me Pippi."

"I'm Coorah," the girl frog told her. "Did one of

them bite you?" she asked, examining the wound. "This doesn't look like a scorpion mark."

Pippi would've answered, but a sudden realization almost took her breath away. "Oh! You must be Darel!" she told the brawny frog. "I've heard so much about you. We need your help. We're in trouble. The Stargazer said—"

"I'm not Darel," the boy frog said. "I'm Gurnugan. Everyone calls *me* Gee."

"Oh!" Pippi said, curling her bill in embarrassment. "Of course. I've heard of you, too. You're Darel's sidekick."

Coorah gave a croak of frog laughter as she bandaged Pippi's wound with a clay wattle leaf. "His sidekick!"

A tree frog with white lips, who was watching from a branch above, called out, "Darel's the warrior, and Gee's the wart!"

"I'm sorry," Pippi told Gee. "I didn't mean anything." She knew what it felt like to be teased.

"Don't worry about them," he said, lifting his chin. "They're just jealous. Now, what were you saying about being in trouble? Are the scorps and spiders bothering you?"

Pippi wrinkled her bill. "Not them. The ghost bats. That's what bit me."

Gee looked at Coorah, but she shook her head and said, "I haven't heard about them."

"You'd better come to the village," Gee told Pippi. "Talk to Chief Olba. She'll know what to do."

"The village in the Amphibilands?" Pippi asked, suddenly excited.

"Of course!" Coorah told her, smiling.

"Are we close?"

"It's a hundred leaps away. Those scorps have been blundering up against the Veil for days."

Pippi peered into the distance, but didn't see anything. "Will Darel be there? The Stargazer says we need Darel."

"He's gone," Gee told her.

"Oh," she said. "Where is he?"

Gee's throat bulged thoughtfully. "I wish I knew."

4

IN THE COOL FOOTHILLS, A PAIR OF GREEN parrots with red beaks darted around a craggy tree. Darel watched them for a moment, enjoying the flash of color, then turned back toward the still-distant peaks of the Snowy Mountains.

Behind him, the outback stretched for endless barren miles under the relentless sun, but here a chill wind blew. Darel narrowed his bulging eyes at the cold, slitted his nostrils, and gripped the reins tighter as his mount swayed beneath him.

Then he almost grinned, despite the chill. His mount. His *giant* mount. His giant *armored, fork-tongued* mount.

He couldn't believe what he was riding.

A Komodo dragon.

He couldn't wait to tell Gee. Not that Gee would believe him. On the other toe pad, Darel couldn't believe a lot of this himself. That he'd defeated Lord

Marmoo . . . that he'd saved the Amphibilands . . . and especially that he was on a quest with the Kulipari. Maybe he was still an ordinary wood frog, without the poison that gave the Kulipari their powers, but even so, he was a member of the squad now. Just like his father had been.

Of course, his father had been a Kulipari squad leader, while Darel was still mostly a . . . tagalong. But that didn't bother him. At least not *much*.

And he'd gotten to know the squad over the past few weeks. Burnu, the leader, riding in front with his boomerangs crisscrossed on his back, was brave and cocky. The squad archer, Dingo, was superfast and superaccurate and superchatty. The biggest of the Kulipari was Ponto. He was strong enough to uproot a tree when he used his power, but he was also a talented healer. And Quoba, bringing up the rear with her staff, was the scout. She could move as quietly as mist, and flitted over the ground like a shadow.

Then there was Darel . . . the wood frog with no weapon except his father's old dagger, and no power except his mother's sense of hard work. Still, it had been enough to beat Lord Marmoo.

Another cold breeze drifted down from the mountains, and he stroked his Komodo dragon's rough head. "Don't worry," he told the huge beast. "We'll stay warm somehow." The dragon's scales were as hard as armor, but they didn't ward off the cold.

"Hey!" Dingo croaked, from beside him. "What do you get when you freeze a frog?"

"Us," Ponto grunted unhappily, hopping along-side. He was the only one not riding a dragon. Good thing his legs were so long and strong that he could keep up.

"A hopsicle!" Dingo said, standing on her dragon's back like she was surfing.

"You're laughing now," Ponto told her. "But wait until we reach the snow."

Darel looked toward the mountains again. "I've never even seen snow."

"Because you're not stupid," Ponto grunted. "Frogs are cold-blooded."

"Then we should *love* the cold!" Dingo ribbeted. "Stop moping, Ponto. You're just grumpy because you're not riding a dragon."

"Crocodiles are one thing," Ponto grumbled. "Whoever heard of riding *dragons*? I'm telling you, it's not right."

The Komodos had washed ashore in the Turtle Coves after a big monsoon—and they'd immediately taken to the frogs, wordlessly offering themselves as mounts. Darel secretly thought that they found frogs funny. He'd caught a glint of amusement in the big lizards' eyes more than once. Maybe that was why Ponto wouldn't ride one.

"None of us should be riding anywhere," Burnu said, from the front, hurling one of his boomerangs into the air. "We should be back at the Amphibilands, kicking scorpion carapace."

"We need Yabber," Darel said firmly.

After the old turtle king died in battle, his apprentice Yabber had become the strongest dreamcaster in the outback. The responsibility worried him, and he'd immediately started running around—well, as fast as a turtle *could* run around—trying to figure out how to defend the Amphibilands.

"*I* don't need anyone," Burnu announced. "I can pound their pincers all by myself."

"Well . . . ," Darel said, thoughtfully. "Maybe Yabber needs *us*."

"Oh." Burnu's boomerang came flashing down from the sky, and he caught it in one hand. "That's okay, then."

"I just wish he needed us somewhere warmer," Ponto grumped.

"Aw, you poor thing." Dingo twirled on her saddle. "Hey, what do you call a sad frog?"

"*You*," Ponto said, "after I knock you off that big lizard."

"'Un-hoppy!'" Dingo cried, then she dodged Ponto's big fist.

5

 AREL SHOOK HIS HEAD, WATCHING Dingo's Komodo dragon lumber away while Ponto chased her past the extra mount they'd brought along for Yabber.

Dingo liked to tease Ponto, which was usually pretty funny, but after the long journey into this strange, chilly landscape, it was getting a little old. They needed to focus on the job. They needed to find Yabber, who'd disappeared into the Snowy Mountains after the defeat of the scorpion hordes.

Yabber had said that with the Veil ripped and the spider queen out for revenge, he needed to retreat to the mountains to hone his powers and meditate on the Rainbow Serpent. He'd promised he'd try to return within a month, and Darel and the Kulipari had spent the first few weeks helping rebuild the villages, chasing away scorpion and spider stragglers, and planning their defenses in case of another attack.

When Yabber hadn't come back after a month, nobody had worried, at first. The turtle dreamcaster could look after himself.

Then they'd started hearing the rumors. A wandering lizard said that Marmoo wasn't dead—or that he'd returned from the dead, stronger than ever. A pair of emus nattered nonsense about Queen Jarrah training a new breed of "devil warrior," but everyone knew emus were total birdbrains.

Finally, a sailfish arrived from the Coves with a message from Yabber's clan, the turtles, claiming that the scorpions were planning a new attack. A huge onslaught, aimed at the rip in the Veil, to bury the Amphibilands in an avalanche of soldiers. And that the spider queen was planning to use the defeat of the Amphibilands as a first step toward spinning her nightcast sorcery across the entire outback.

That was when Chief Olba had decided they needed to find Yabber—and fast. So Darel had kissed his mother and the triplets—his little brothers and sister—good-bye and joined the Kulipari on this trek.

With all that hanging over them, Darel didn't understand how Dingo could goof around so much. He sighed, watching her darting away from Ponto, spinning under her dragon's scaly neck, then popping up on the other side.

"Don't worry about Dingo," Quoba said, suddenly beside him. "She's just trying to keep our spirits up."

"How do you *do* that?" he asked.

"Creep up on you?"

"Well, that too. But I meant, how do you always know what I'm thinking?"

She smiled. "Because I'm usually thinking the same thing."

They rode in silence for a moment. Darel yawned. "I've never been so sleepy."

"Don't close your eyes until we've made a fire," Quoba told him.

"Why not?"

"Like Ponto said, we're cold-blooded. Warm-bloods like koalas and emus make their own heat. They stay warm even when the air is cold. Not us. When the world cools down, we cool down, too."

"Because we're normal," Darel said. "How freaky is it that warm-bloods always have the same temperature?"

Quoba grinned. "I don't know how they live in those fuzzy bodies."

"But the Amphibilands never *freezes*," Darel continued. "What happens to us in the snow?"

"Well, some frogs and turtles snuggle into the mud at the bottom of frozen lakes and stay there all winter. They hibernate. Others—like wood frogs, I think—wait for the frost, then fall asleep and freeze solid."

"Like an *actual* hopsicle?"

Quoba laughed. "Exactly. And when the spring comes, they thaw out."

"That is so cool!" Darel said, his eye bulging. "I can do that?"

"You wood frogs have many hidden talents. There's one problem, though. On the Snowy Mountains, there are places that never thaw. You'd stay frozen forever."

Darel gulped. "Oh."

"So don't fall asleep in the snow, nor in the mountains."

"Gotcha," he said. "I won't."

"And the cold slows us down, making us sluggish and sleepy. I'm not sure we can even tap into our poison in the snow."

"That's not a problem for me," Darel complained. "I don't have any poison to tap into."

"In some ways that makes you stronger," Quoba said in her quiet voice. "Perhaps we rely on our poison too much."

The next morning, as Darel was riding beside the spare mount, an arrow suddenly jabbed into the ground twenty feet from him.

"That's a sign from Dingo!" Burnu said, leaping off his Komodo. "She's seen something!"

Darel followed, and they found Dingo—who'd been scouting the path ahead—crouching beside the tattered remains of a web, her bow in her hand. As Darel eyed the long, dusty web that disappeared into the underbrush on both sides, a sick feeling rose in his stomach.

"That's not a normal web," Burnu said, drawing his boomerangs.

"Looks like a nightcasting." Quoba slipped beside them. "It's a huge circle."

"There's a village in the middle," Dingo said, her face solemn for once. "A wallaby village."

But there was no village. Not anymore. There were only dead crops, dry wells . . . and skeletons. Wallaby skeletons.

"Jarrah must've dried up the springs," Darel said,

wiping tears from his cheeks. "Then used that big web to trap the wallabies inside."

"But why?" Ponto asked.

"Maybe to punish them." Darel swallowed thickly. "Or to test her power, now that King Sergu is dead."

For a moment nobody spoke, remembering the turtle king, who'd died in battle protecting the Amphibilands.

Then Quoba nodded. "Yabber once told me that dreamcasting came from the Rainbow Serpent, cool and healing and life-giving. But nightcasting is the opposite—harsh and deadly and *dry*."

"Figures that Jarrah would use thirst to kill," Ponto said. "And with Sergu gone, there's nothing to stand in her way."

"Except Yabber," Darel said.

"And us," Burnu said.

They traveled for two more days, as the foothills grew into mountains. They stopped every night and ate smoked bogong moths around a campfire. To keep themselves and the Komodo dragons warm, they heated rocks in the fire, then tucked them around their mounts in heavy, bulging saddlebags.

On the third day, they traveled through a craggy

mountain pass as snowflakes swirled from the sky. Cliffs rose on both sides, and Darel was eyeing the high rock walls when, without any warning, the flurry of snow turned into a blinding storm.

He leaned forward, pressing his chest against the warm rocks draped over his saddle. They'd need to stop soon, to light another fire. His eyes closed to slits, and snowflakes brushed his face. Time crept and the warm rocks grew cold, and he felt his Komodo dragon slowing under him. As the storm grew, he peered

sleepily through the curtains of snow and barely saw the dark blotch of Dingo's mount ahead of him on the icy path.

He felt numb and defeated, like they'd never find Yabber, like they'd never leave these mountains alive. He weakly touched the dagger at his hip. His father's dagger. He thought about Gee and Coorah back home, about his mother and his brothers and sister and Chief Olba. He felt the snow on his cloak freezing the fabric to his back as the rolling motion of the Komodo dragon rocked him gently.

He closed his eyes for one moment . . .

. . . and when he opened them, the air smelled of smoke, and a gray wolf was about to bite his head off.

6

EAR MADE DAREL'S EYES BULGE. HE didn't blink; he didn't even breathe, afraid that if he moved, the gray wolf would rip his throat out. He just stared at the black eyes gleaming and brown fur bristling and . . .

And as he came fully awake, he saw that the creature wasn't a wolf at all.

In fact, it was tiny.

Like a mouse.

He felt its four teeny paws standing on his chest, and realized that its fuzzy face was just a few inches from his—that's why it looked so big. Relief flooded through him, and he smiled at the little creature. It licked its paw, then dashed off his chest, its long pink tail trailing behind.

"Good morning, good morning, good morning!" Yabber called, his voice warm and echoing. "You look much better, Darel! In the very green of health. Except, of course, you're browner than you are green, or a sort of sea-bark color, or would you call that 'wombat-olive,' or perhaps—"

"Yabber!" Darel said, croaking in pleasure and grinning at the long-neck turtle. "What happened? Where are we? Is everyone okay?"

He looked around and found himself in a smoky cave like nothing he'd ever seen—like nothing he'd ever even imagined. Hundreds of stalactites and stalagmites shimmered with a red glow. They hung from the arching cave roof and rose like twisty tree trunks from the floor. Steam wafted from a pool of slushy water, and Yabber stood near the warmth of a flickering campfire, fiddling with a bunch of smoked fish dangling from a line. A dozen of the tiny mouse-things nervously perched on his shell.

Yabber craned his long neck toward Darel. "Oh, yes, you look much better now. All thawed out. Well! I told my friends here that you weren't usually so stiff."

Darel blinked. "Your friends?"

"They're mountain pygmy possums. Aren't they sweet? They found you in the snow, and—"

A crunching sound echoed through the cave, and the possums scattered, disappearing into the shadows.

"And they are very shy," Yabber continued. "Now,

then, what did you ask? Oh, yes. The answers are as follows: you froze . . . in a cave . . . and yes."

"Yabber," Darel said, rubbing his head and hopping closer to the fire. "Slow down. I can't even remember what questions I asked."

"Whaaat happennned?" Yabber said, speaking extremely slowly. "You frrrrrroze. Where are weeeeee? In a caaaaaave. And yesssss, everyone is oooookay."

"Oh. Good."

"And I am supposed to tell you to drink the potion in that flask," Yabber said, speaking as fast as ever and gesturing to a leather canteen near Darel. "Ponto made it. To help you heal. Drink up! You'll feel better in no time."

Darel grabbed the flask. He sniffed, wrinkled his nose, then drank. It tasted like lemon-flavored grub.

The crunching sounded again, and Burnu hopped toward the fire. "Cold out there," he told Yabber, then glanced at Darel. "So you woke the lazy wood frog, did you?"

"He just needed a little warming," Yabber told him. "Nothing to worry about. Of course, if the possums hadn't found you . . ."

"*We* were fine!" Burnu said.

"You were a fine-looking collection of ice sculptures," Yabber said. "Perched atop Komodo statues."

"We *all* froze?" Darel asked, turning so the fire could warm his butt.

"Don't listen to the turtle," Burnu said. "You're the only one who froze. The rest of us are real Kulipari. We tapped into our poison."

"And we were still as slow as slugs and as weak as moths," Quoba said, slipping from the shadows beside Yabber. "Our poison doesn't work well in the cold."

"Would someone *please* tell me what happened?" Darel said, taking another swig of the lemon-grubby potion.

"It's very simple," Yabber told him. "You froze. The others were stumbling around lost and exhausted in a snowstorm. The possums found you, and brought you here."

"Where is 'here,' exactly?"

"One of the Yarrangobilly caves," Quoba said. "High in the mountains. It's beautiful, isn't it?"

"It's a *cave*," Burnu said. "It's not beautiful. It's just cold."

"Oddly cold," Yabber told him. "*Too* cold. I wonder if Jarrah is responsible."

"You think she made the snowstorm?" Darel asked, slitting his nostrils in suspicion. "Can she do that?"

"I don't know." Yabber lowered his head to sniff

a smoked fish. "But I've felt her gaining power for weeks now. We are connected somehow, Jarrah and I—perhaps simply because we were King Sergu's best students. Of course, I was always his star pupil, if I do say so myself. Not sure if I ever mentioned that, but—"

"Maybe once or twice," Darel interrupted. "Did the others tell you about the wallaby village we saw?"

"The dead village?" Yabber sighed. "Yes. I think Marmoo is after the Amphibilands, but Jarrah's playing a deeper game. She killed King Sergu because she wants to weave her nightcast web over the entire outback, and he was one of the few powerful enough to stop her."

"And now she's even stronger than before?"

"Much stronger. Her nightcasting skills are growing fast . . ." Yabber arched his neck. "But so are mine. Well, not my *night*casting skills! I've still only got four legs. Not a spider, last I checked—though I'd look extremely handsome in silk. No, I mean, my *dream*-casting skills."

"Well, that's why you came here, right?" Burnu asked him. "To hone your powers."

"Oh, yes. Yes, yes, yes!" Yabber considered. "Well, not exactly."

"What? You said you needed some time alone, to—" Burnu looked at Quoba. "What'd he call it?"

"Dream deeper," Quoba said.

"Well . . ." Yabber arched his long neck again. "Yes. I needed to commune with the Rainbow Serpent, the source of all dreamcasting powers."

"What does 'commune' mean?" Darel asked.

"To connect with," Yabber explained. "The Serpent is mysterious, though—only the platypuses even halfway understand it. Well, perhaps King Sergu did, as well."

"He did?"

"I think he suggested that I practice my dreamcasting in *these* caves for a reason."

"Maybe because they're in the middle of nowhere?" Burnu asked. "Nobody will bother you here?"

"That's what I thought, at first," Yabber told him. "Then I found something deep in the caves. I suspect the king mentioned these particular caves knowing that I wouldn't come until after he'd . . . well, died. And only if we were in trouble."

"You think he wanted you to come here?" Burnu asked. "And find this strange thing?"

"Who found what now?" Dingo asked, leaping into the cavern and lowering the hood of her cloak.

"Yabber," Burnu told her. "He found something, deeper in the caves."

Ponto hopped one-footed behind her, trying to shake the snow out of his toes. "Let me guess. He found . . . more dirt."

"And darkness!" Dingo bulged her eyes at Yabber. "You found more cave, didn't you?"

"Of course I found more cave! But on the walls, there are drawings. Mysterious symbols and—"

"You found *art*?" Burnu grumbled. "There are scorpions to squish and spiders to squash, and we're sitting in a cave freezing our warts off. This is ridiculous. How are the dragons, Ponto?"

Ponto warmed his finger pads by the fire. "They're good. They're ready to move."

"Then let's go," Burnu said. "The Amphibilands needs us. I'm a Kulipari, trained to fight, not to muck around underground like a worm."

"Maybe you're a spelunker," Dingo said.

He frowned at her. "What did you call me?"

"A spelunker."

"You're the spelunk-head."

"Spelunk*er*," she said. "It means cave diver."

"Stop talking gibberish," Burnu snapped, drawing one of his boomerangs.

"You two settle down," Ponto told them, in his deep voice.

"You must see the drawings before you rush off!" Yabber interrupted. "They are quite extraordinary, obviously inspired by the Rainbow Serpent. In fact, I rather suspect they are the key to our future—to the future of the entire outback."

"Or they're the work of a really artistic worm," Burnu muttered.

"Well, come along, and see for yourself!"

For some reason, Ponto and Quoba both looked at Darel, like it was his decision. "Uh, we should have a look," Darel said.

"Fine," Burnu sighed. "But after that, we're all heading home. There's a battle brewing, and I don't want to miss any of it."

"I'm with Burnu," Dingo muttered. "The big spelunk-head."

Burnu threw his boomerang at her.

She backflipped away, and the boomerang dinged off Yabber's shell, then ricocheted into a stalactite. Ponto snatched it from the air and refused to return it until Burnu promised he wouldn't throw it again.

Darel flicked his inner eyelid in amusement at Quoba as they followed Yabber toward the back of the cave. But a second later, he furrowed his brow in thought. Mysterious symbols, inspired by the Rainbow Serpent, deep in a cave that King Sergu expected Yabber to visit in case of trouble?

Who'd drawn them? How long ago? And how could they help keep the outback safe?

COMMANDER PIGO PATROLLED THE corridor outside Lord Marmoo's chamber, scuttling along the boulders of the spider queen's castle. Spider guards and servants bowed and scurried aside when they saw him, creeping onto the walls or ceiling.

As second-in-command of the scorpion army, Pigo was not someone they wanted to anger. Only the spider queen's ladies-in-waiting—her three new assistant nightcasters—and Queen Jarrah herself were unafraid of him.

When Pigo turned, he saw the queen at the far end of the hallway, tall and regal. "Ah, Commander," she said, slinking closer, her ladies following behind her. "How is Lord Marmoo? Is he . . . himself again?"

Pigo bowed with his front legs. "I haven't heard from him in some time, your majesty."

"Still hiding away, is he?"

"I expect him to come out soon."

"There's no need to wait," Jarrah said, with a cold smile. "I'll simply let myself in."

"Er," Pigo said, unsure. On the one pincer, he knew that Marmoo hated Jarrah and didn't want her to see him in his current state. On the other pincer, he knew that Marmoo needed Jarrah—at least for a short time longer.

"Of course, your majesty," he said finally, and he opened the door for her and her ladies-in-waiting.

The rough rock walls and floor of the chamber were hidden by sheets of spider silk, woven into tapestries and carpets. Two scorpion warriors stood guard, their main eyes and side eyes alert as they bowed in greeting. A dry breeze blew in from the thin slit of a window, and a nightcasted web in the corner of the ceiling shone with as much light as half a dozen torches. A table was laden with roast rat tails and caterpillar stew.

And in the center of the room stood a massive scorpion.

Lord Marmoo. Perfectly still. Like a statue.

His stinger was frozen; his pincers were motionless. The two eyes in the front of his head and the three pairs on the sides all stared straight ahead.

Then a soft tearing sound broke the silence. A jagged line appeared at Marmoo's shoulders, a deep crack ripping his carapace in two from the inside.

The ladies-in-waiting gasped and skittered backward, but the queen strolled forward for a closer look as the split in Marmoo's thick carapace deepened.

"Wh-wh-what's happening?" one lady-in-waiting stammered.

"He's molting," Pigo explained. "It's how we grow."

"But scorpions don't molt after they're fully grown!"

"Not usually," the queen said, running one of her spidery fingers down the unmoving stinger. "But Marmoo is different now. My nightcasting magic gave him the strength and vigor of youth. And look . . ."

The split in Marmoo's carapace spread wider, past his shoulders to the bottoms of his pincers. One of his legs trembled, then another. His stinger shifted the tiniest bit.

With a sudden pop, another long crack appeared, running down his side. A ragged hole opened in his scarred black carapace, just between his shoulders . . . and something crawled out from inside it.

First one pincer appeared, opening slowly and

snapping closed. Then two legs scrabbled at the edges of the hole, pulling and tugging. A moment later, Marmoo's head emerged, then his body and his legs and finally his stinger, long and serpentine, the tip shining with poison.

He stretched, and this time even Queen Jarrah took a tiny step backward.

Marmoo was almost twice as large as he'd been before. His eyes shone brightly, and his pincers were lined with razor-like serrations. His carapace was thicker, ridged with scales, completely unscratched, and a different color than before. He was now a shade of pale gray.

He rolled his shoulders and stretched each leg, then slowly turned toward the others, looming over them so the room suddenly felt too small, even to Pigo.

"Oh, very nice," he said, smashing the wooden table in half with one blow of his pincer. "Well done, Jarrah. I am stronger than ever."

"How kind of you to say that," she murmured, stepping closer again. "But while you're stronger, your shell is still soft and pale."

"Pigo!" Marmoo snapped, unwilling to believe it. "Strike me."

Without any hesitation, Pigo lashed out with a pincer. Lord Marmoo didn't even flinch when Pigo's pincer slashed through his side. He only frowned, because the sharp edge cut so easily through his armor—his new pale carapace was as soft as frogskin.

"That's my first scar in this new carapace," he told Pigo, lowering his head to watch his blood trickle to the floor. "I'm glad it was you who gave it to me, Commander."

"An honor, m'lord," Pigo said, bowing.

Marmoo swiveled his side eyes toward the spider queen. "How soon before it hardens?"

"Well, Lord Marmoo," she murmured. "Your new strength is born from my magic. It is only my webbing that will harden your shell."

Marmoo's mouthparts clicked. "Then spin your web and make my armor so thick that not even the Kulipari can pierce it."

"Oh, I will." She prowled toward the door. "But not today. I only stopped in to see if you'd . . . come out of your shell."

The ladies-in-waiting giggled at the little joke, which made Pigo want to sting them all.

"And to tell you," Jarrah continued, glancing back

from the doorway, "that I've been tracking that repulsive long-neck turtle."

"The dreamcaster?"

"Yes, the one called 'Yabber.'" She shuddered. "Even his name makes me ill. He ran from the Amphibilands—I know that much. And I am about to find his exact location. Here, come along."

As she sidled from the room, Pigo met Lord Marmoo's eyes and saw the rage in them. His lordship didn't like being ordered around like a pet—and he *hated* weakness, so being stuck with a vulnerable carapace must have enraged him. But an instant later, the anger disappeared. His lordship also knew how to wait for the right moment to strike.

Pigo and the guards scuttled along behind Lord Marmoo as the spider queen led them higher in the castle, finally emerging on a craggy stone roof. A squeaky buzzing grew louder as they climbed to a platform atop the highest boulder, where a huge spiderweb stretched between two rock pilings.

A hundred trapped flies buzzed in the web, their wings beating in helpless terror. Pigo squeezed his mouthparts together and scanned the surrounding countryside, the mines and the swamp and the desert beyond. He couldn't wait to return to the sand, to escape the spider castle, with its sticky webs and sly whispers.

"Step a little closer," Queen Jarrah told Marmoo. "Look into the web."

As Marmoo approached, Jarrah took a terrified butterfly from one of her ladies-in-waiting and sank her fangs into it. The butterfly stopped moving as she pumped it full of poison. She circled the spiderweb, drawing a silken thread from her spinnerets and wrapping the dead butterfly tightly, humming a strange song that made Pigo's head ache.

When the butterfly was completely encased in a silken ball, Jarrah drew back her arm and hurled the ball into the center of the web. The web trembled and a glimmer of magic swirled along all the strands, killing every fly it touched.

Then the web grew lighter and lighter until it was a pure white circle. Slowly, shapes appeared in the whiteness. With a sudden jerk, Pigo realized that the web had turned into a sort of window, and they were looking at a landscape. It wasn't just blank whiteness; it was *snow*.

A snowy cliff of some sort. The picture shifted, and dark blotches appeared, until finally they saw the outline of a huge jagged shape.

"The Snowy Mountains," Marmoo said.

"Ahh," Jarrah breathed. "So *that* is where Yabber is hiding."

"That's no place for a turtle."

She frowned fiercely. "It is where they dream about the Rainbow Serpent. Hmm. So that foul water snake has chosen sides?"

"What can the Serpent do?" Marmoo asked. "Is it powerful?"

"It is as old as time," she told him. "Wise and cunning . . . but not powerful, no. It only acts through lesser creatures. Frogs and turtles, platypuses and other pond scum." She eyed the snowy picture. "I'll send my strike force at once."

"Your what?" Marmoo asked.

"I've been gathering soldiers while you were recovering. The blue-banded bees joined my army, and the ghost bats are taking care of a little problem for me as we speak."

"You're sending bats to the Snowy Mountains?"

"No, no," she replied. "I sent them after the platypus village, just in case. The Rainbow Serpent's meddling doesn't come as a complete surprise, and nobody understands the Serpent as well as the duck-billed freaks. Well, no matter. I'll stop the Serpent's interference before it even begins. The ghost bats will finish the platypuses, and I have another squad for the mountains."

She nodded to a spider soldier, who pulled a lever that opened a trapdoor in the floor. With the creaking of chains, a square of stone shifted, revealing a pit.

A low hissing sounded from inside, and Pigo side-stepped closer to Marmoo while the guards reached automatically for their battle nets.

"Oh, they're quite tame," Jarrah told Pigo, slinking toward the pit. "And absolutely loyal."

Marmoo peered into the pit, then clicked one of his pincers in admiration. "Very impressive. Even that jabbering idiot of a dreamcaster cannot survive a squad of *taipan* snakes."

"And they're not even my fiercest new troops."

"No?" Marmoo asked. "You have more?"

"I have *worse*." Jarrah smiled hungrily. "I call them my little devils."

8

PIPPI'S SENSITIVE BILL TINGLED LIKE crazy when the frogs escorted her through the Veil, but nothing else seemed to change.

Then she realized that while the rolling hills on the edge of the forest didn't look any different, she suddenly had a much better sense of where she was. The Veil must have been disorienting her. Now she knew that the platypus tribe was behind her and the coast was ahead. The scent of eucalyptus and fresh water that wafted through the shrubbery gave her a mental picture of her surroundings.

"Do you smell that?" Gee asked.

She nodded. "Is it the Amphibilands?"

"That's home." He offered her a honey-roasted snail. "You want one?"

She nodded again. "Please."

It was sweet and chewy. Not as tasty for a platypus as water worms and crayfish, but still pretty good. She smacked her bill together to keep the sticky honey from gluing her mouth shut and noticed Gee watching her closely.

"What's wrong?" she asked. "Am I doing something wrong?"

"I've just never seen a platypus before. That's funny, what you do with your beak after you eat." He smacked his froggy lips together. "Like this."

"It's not a beak—it's a bill." She licked more honey away. "And we *don't* do that."

He teasingly inflated his throat. "You just did it again!"

"I did not!"

"Did too."

"Well, at least I don't do *this*," she said, bulging out her cheeks.

Gee snorted. "Neither do I."

"Do too!"

"Do not."

"Hey, look at me everyone!" Pippi called. "I'm Gee!"

She puffed out her cheeks and looked to Coorah and Arabanoo, the white-lipped tree frog.

"Not your *cheeks*." Arabanoo grinned and bulged out his throat. "Your throat."

Pippi squinched her face, trying to make her throat puff up, but she only made herself dizzy. The frogs laughed, then started inflating their cheeks as everyone headed into the fringes of the eucalyptus forest.

They headed downhill, with the frogs occasionally shooting their tongues out to catch flies. They paused at one point to watch Pippi catch worms using the tingly sense in her bill. They were pretty impressed,

which she thought was silly, so she asked them to tell her stories about the war.

They all joined in as they walked on, telling her about battling scorpions and spiders. The scent of water grew stronger, and the sun lowered through the eucalyptus trees. When they passed a small leafy village, a few young frogs with itty-bitty tails hopped after them, staring with bulging eyes at Pippi. She felt shy but also a little proud, because Gee kept introducing her as "Okipippi, a heroic scout from the platypus tribe."

Finally, Coorah hopped up beside her. "See that ahead? Past that bridge and the worm farm? That's the main village. It's where Chief Olba lives."

"Oh." Pippi swished her tail, nervous about meeting the chief. "What's she like?"

"She's nice. She'll like you."

Pippi wasn't so sure. She was a long way from home, and everything looked strange and different.

"That reminds me of another story about Darel," Coorah told her. "He once knocked down half the marketplace."

"No way!"

Coorah nodded. "He and Arabanoo were fighting,

and they knocked over a huge stack of barrels. The barrels rolled downhill and smashed everything."

"I was beating him, too!" Arabanoo ribbeted, from farther along the path.

"So as long as you don't knock down the village hall," Coorah told Pippi, with a wink, "you'll be okay."

Pippi smiled, and a few minutes later they entered the central frog village. It was ten times as big as the platypus tribe's riverbank warren. A whole family of frogs seemed to live in every tree branch, and bigger frogs with deep voices watched from the mouths of burrows that looked pretty comfy. The buildings were shingled with leaves and twigs and sprawled low around the tree trunks. The air smelled moist and mossy, and tiny ponds looked just the right size for Pippi to take a relaxing swim in.

The town hall, though, was grand and lofty, which made her nervous again.

"Are we going in there?" she asked Gee.

"Well, let's try next door first."

A pretty little leaf house stood in the shadow of the town hall. It looked much less intimidating, so Pippi nodded eagerly. When Coorah opened the gate in the fence, Pippi ambled through. Then she stopped short. A frail old frog with unhealthy-looking pale skin was sitting on a tree-stump chair on the porch, watching her with white eyes.

"Now, what is *this*?" the old frog asked, peering at Pippi with his clouded eyes. "A platypus! I haven't seen one of you in years! Are you from the riverbend?"

"Oh!" Pippi said, surprised that he knew of her tribe. "You've heard of us? Yes, I—I—I'm Pippi."

The elderly frog inflated his throat. "They call me Old Jir."

"He used to be a Kulipari," Gee told her. "A real hero."

"Then I used too much of my poison," Old Jir said, shaking his head sadly. "If a Kulipari overuses his power, he loses it—forever. He turns pale and weak, like me."

"You might be pale," Gee said. "But you're not *weak*."

Old Jir slitted his nostrils. "When I was your age, Gurnugan, I could juggle boulders." He looked back to Pippi. "I did some traveling in my younger days and once met a platypus they called the Stargazer, and she—"

"Oooh!" Pippi said, clapping her paws. "You know

the Stargazer? She's taught me since I was a little pup, all the legends and dances and—"

Coorah touched her arm. "Let's meet the chief first, then you can chat with Old Jir later."

"How come healers are so bossy?" Old Jir grumped, squinting at Coorah.

"Because our patients always test our patience," Coorah said primly.

Old Jir snorted a laugh and said, "She's right. We'll talk later, Pippi. The Stargazer's a grand old friend of mine. We used to race when she was a girl—she'd zip down the mudslide to the water, and I'd leap from the riverbank, to see who'd splash in first."

"No!" Pippi gasped. She couldn't imagine the dignified gray-furred Stargazer sliding down the mud. "The Stargazer would ride the mudslide?"

"She was fast, too," Old Jir said, stroking his chin with his toe pads. "Now inside with you, pup. Time to see the chief."

"Yes, sir," Pippi said.

"Chief!" Old Jir bellowed, opening the door for Pippi. "Got a special guest for you!"

"You talk to the chief," Gee told Pippi. "Coorah and I have to hop along and see our parents."

Pippi felt her bill droop in dismay. "O-o-okay."

"We'll come get you later," Coorah said. "I promise."

Pippi nodded, gathered her courage, and stepped through the doorway.

The living room of the leaf house was pretty and cluttered. A lamp glowed on a plank table beside a vase of flowers, and the scent of baking wafted from deeper in the house. It reminded Pippi a little of her burrow, which made her smile. "Hello?" she called.

There was no answer, so she went farther inside and saw a leafy archway leading into the town hall. She figured the chief was in there, waiting on a throne, surrounded by guards with swords and shields. She was working up the courage to step through when a faint ribbet of welcome sounded behind her.

Pippi turned and saw an older frog with glossy black skin and a red dot on her forehead. "Oh!" she said. "I didn't see you there."

The frog patted her bulging potbelly. "Well, I'm pretty hard to spot."

Pippi giggled. "You should try being a platypus. We stand out everywhere."

"Ha! Very true!" the older frog said. "You're a

clever tribe, though. And *nobody* understands the Rainbow Serpent as well as your Stargazer."

"You know the Stargazer, too?"

The frog cocked her head. "Have you been talking to Old Jir?"

"I just met him," Pippi said.

"Well, I've never met the Stargazer," the frog said, "but I've heard of her. Old King Sergu—the turtle king—used to tell stories about the platypus stargazers. He said a new one is born every generation and they're extremely wise." She grinned froggishly. "Even if they're sometimes . . . foggy-headed dreamers."

"He said *that*?" Pippi asked, pursing her bill. "The old turtle king?"

"He did indeed," the frog said.

But sometimes others called *her* a foggy-headed dreamer! Pippi thought about that but didn't say anything. She sat there, slowly swishing her tail back and forth.

"Now, then," the pudgy frog said suddenly, "is there something I can do for you?"

Pippi looked up, startled. "Well," she said, "I'm supposed to talk to the chief, but I'm feeling a little shy."

"Why don't you come into the kitchen and tell me all about it?"

"Um . . ." Pippi hesitated, eyeing the archway into the town hall.

"I just baked some clam muffins," the frog said. "Fresh from the oven, if you'd like a taste."

"Well, maybe I'll just have *one*."

They went into the kitchen, where the frog gave Pippi two clam muffins on a plate, then sat beside her and sipped herbal tea. The muffins were delicious, and while Pippi was eating, the pudgy frog asked what brought her to the Amphibilands.

Between bites, Pippi told the story. The frog's forehead furrowed in concern when Pippi got to the part about the ghost bats, and she looked even more concerned when Pippi said, "And the Stargazer said there are scary new threats rising against us—and against you, here, in the Amphibilands."

"Threats?" the old frog asked.

Pippi nodded, feeling a sudden urgency. "I really should go talk to Chief Olba! But it's been *so* nice to meet you. You've been very kind."

"Didn't I introduce myself?" the frog said. "I'm sorry. *I'm* Chief Olba."

"R-r-really?" Pippi asked, blinking in surprise. "But these muffins are so tasty! I thought you were the cook."

Chief Olba inflated her throat in amusement. "That's the nicest thing anyone's said to me in a very long time."

Pippi's bill curled in embarrassment. "I'm sorry, ma'am! I didn't know."

"That's quite all right. Another muffin? Now, dear, tell me exactly what the Stargazer said."

"She—she said war is coming, a battle for water. The final battle. The spider queen was trying to kill us, because we listen to the Rainbow Serpent. She said there was a danger from the air, and when the ghost bats came, I realized she'd been talking about them. I—I—I don't even want to think about what's happened since I left. My sister and mother and father. All my cousins and friends and . . ." Pippi swallowed. "We can't fight off bats. They're too fast and too mean and they *fly*."

Chief Olba thought for a moment, staring into her teacup. "Did the Stargazer say what you should do about it?"

"Not exactly," Pippi said. "But she said we need your help. We need the Amphibilands."

"Well, of course we'll help you. What do you need?"

"We need Darel and the Kulipari," Pippi said. "That's what the Stargazer told me. Except . . . she doesn't only call him 'Darel.' "

"No? What else does she call him?"

"The Blue Sky King."

IGO SHADOWED LORD MARMOO through the swamp at the foot of the spider queen's mountain, still amazed by his lordship's size and strength. Marmoo lashed with his stinger and split a shaggy-barked blackwood tree in half. He splashed through the murky water. His side eyes shifted slightly, and his pincer whipped into the shadows.

A spider's shrill scream sounded—then stopped suddenly, as Marmoo's pincer chopped him in half.

"I'm faster, too," Marmoo said, feeling a cold rush of satisfaction. "Bigger, stronger, faster."

"Yes, my lord," Commander Pigo said, skittering closer.

Pigo's mouthparts moved into an expression of disgust at the stench that wafted from the tainted water. That's why they needed the Amphibilands. Not merely because they hated the croakers, but because the froglands were the richest source of fresh, *pure* water—and even desert creatures knew that water was the source of life.

Pigo watched Lord Marmoo with his side eyes. Despite his soft carapace, Lord Marmoo remained the most dangerous creature in the outback . . . and the best chance of tearing down the Veil and taking all that clean water.

"Shall we release another spider for you to hunt, my lord?" he asked.

Marmoo shook his head. "Four is enough for this evening. I don't want to kill *all* the spiders working in Jarrah's mines, though I'm sure she won't miss a few."

"Yes, m'lord."

Marmoo headed for the path. "Although there's no telling with her. She thinks she rules me now, because she healed me. Well, if it weren't for *her* failed night-casting, I would've beaten the frogs once and for all. She doesn't own me—she *owes* me."

Pigo's legs moved quickly to catch up with Marmoo's much longer stride. "And, erm, your carapace?"

Marmoo tossed the spider's body deeper into the swamp, where it disappeared with a splash. "Still soft as an egg yolk. I'm stronger, faster, bigger, but . . . vulnerable. And I refuse to accept weakness, Pigo—not in others, not in myself. The spider queen will pay for this. I'll snap all her legs off if she doesn't harden my carapace soon."

"Yes, m'lord."

"And when she *does* harden it?" Marmoo bared his fangs. "I'll still snap her legs off."

"All you need is her silk wrapped around you," Pigo told him. "And a drop of her poison."

Marmoo worked his mouthparts thoughtfully. "How do you know?"

"I overheard her ladies-in-waiting gossiping. One said it's hardly even a nightcasting, just Jarrah's web and poison. It should only take a few moments. In fact, m'lord, even without her magic your carapace will harden by itself . . . eventually."

"Is that so?" Marmoo asked, a dangerous glint in his main eyes. "She told me otherwise. She said I needed her."

"I expect, m'lord, that she lied."

"Good to know. So . . . you have been spying on the spiders, Commander?"

Pigo lowered his head. "Yes, m'lord."

"Good." Marmoo clasped him on the armored shoulder. "Keep it up."

The scorpion lord turned and marched through the swamp, with Pigo following respectfully behind. Three soldiers fell in with Pigo at the miner's village, where trembling spiders accidentally unspooled wads of silk at the sight of Marmoo, so much larger and stronger than before, with that eerie pale carapace.

Marmoo snapped his pincers, and the miners scurried back into the tunnels.

The squad climbed the rocky path toward the mountaintop, and soon the castle came into view. Hundreds of boulders were stacked together and draped in silk. The queen and her court lived in the ornate cracks and crevices.

As Marmoo led the way across the drawbridge that spanned the wide, sticky "moat" of spiderwebs, Pigo spotted Queen Jarrah and her ladies scurrying across one of the exterior walls. The spiders treated walls and ceilings just like floors, and Pigo watched the queen scuttling toward the castle roof, where she did much of her nightcasting.

"My lord," he murmured, shifting his main eyes upward.

Marmoo followed his gaze, snapped a pincer, then skittered through the castle's craggy hallways and up the rough-hewn stairs. By the time Pigo followed him onto the rooftop, Jarrah had already finished her spell. Silken bundles of dead insects scattered the stones at her feet, and she finished sucking the blood from another before tossing it aside.

"Ah, Lord Marmoo," the queen said, licking her lips. "Every time I see you, I'm surprised anew at how large you've grown."

Marmoo crossed toward the spiderweb stretched between two boulders, shimmering with a sickly glow. "I hope your nightcasting was successful?"

"Of course. Shall I tell you what I learned?"

Marmoo ground his mouthparts. Pigo knew that his lordship hated that Jarrah always made him ask, instead of simply telling him what he needed to know. It was her way of asserting her superiority.

"Please do," Marmoo said, playing along . . . for now.

"I've pinpointed Yabber and sent the information to my troops. They're almost there, almost upon him. And the Kulipari, as well."

"They're in the Snowy Mountains?"

She nodded. "In a cave. The turtle king once mentioned it to me, a deep cave where the ancients doodled Serpentine idiocy on the walls. Except, of course, the turtle thought the drawings revealed great insight and wisdom." She showed her fangs in a cold smile. "I suppose Yabber hopes to use the drawings against us."

"So what will you do, Queen Jarrah?" Pigo asked.

"I'll bury him," she said. "I'll bury them all."

"You never fought the Kulipari," Marmoo said, his stinger coiling. "I'm not so sure that the taipan snakes will defeat them."

"Ah, but I didn't only send the taipan. I have another surprise in store."

Marmoo nodded, considering the queen. And Pigo knew him well enough to follow his thoughts: The queen was manipulative, with her petty games, but also far more dangerous than she appeared.

10

TWO DARK PASSAGES OPENED IN the back of the cave, and Yabber muttered to himself before picking the one on the right. He headed into a cavern filled with what looked like stone mushrooms, most of them taller than Darel, then squeezed through a crack in the wall that led into a narrow, twisting tunnel.

After a dozen turns, the rock walls narrowed so much that Ponto had to use his considerable strength to turn Yabber sideways, to fit his shell between them.

"This is much easier with you than with the possums," Yabber said. "It took a hundred of them to squeeze me through!"

They followed the winding passageway deeper into the mountain, and Darel found himself glancing nervously upward, imagining the millions of tons of earth above him. If all that dirt and rock came crashing down, it would smoosh him like an egg.

At a junction of six passages, Yabber paused and hummed to himself, then seemed to nod off for a moment.

"Is it naptime already?" Dingo asked. "Hey, Ponto, will you tuck me in?"

"He's dreamcasting," Darel told her.

Burnu snorted. "He's *yawn*casting."

"Ah!" Yabber said, suddenly. "This one."

He chose a passage that was basically a hole in the floor, and they lowered themselves inside, one by one. After another few minutes of crawling through winding tunnels, they emerged into a chilly circular chamber with a dome-like roof.

"Bring the torches close to the wall," Yabber told them, gesturing grandly. "And behold!"

At first, the painted markings on the wall looked to Darel like a random pattern of lines and circles and colors. Then he started to make out shapes. Red and yellow stencils of paws of various animals—kangaroos, rats, wallabies—and the tracks of ostriches and snakes and even an ant trail. There were figures, too: A mass of spiders and scorpions swarmed near a few lizards and a cloud of tiny flying creatures. A turtle with yellow eyes stood with dozens of frogs. Frogs of many colors—Kulipari?—and some frogs with no color at all, just outlined, which made Darel think they were ex-Kulipari who'd lost their poison.

"What does it mean?" Darel asked Yabber.

"I'm not exactly sure," Yabber admitted. "I only discovered this chamber a few days ago, and I've been trying to answer that question ever since. It seems to be a story or . . . instructions."

"Wait!" Dingo bent forward, peering closely at an orange shape.

"Did you find something?" Darel asked, eagerly.

"I found an important question. What's orange and sounds like a parrot?"

"I don't know," Quoba said, stepping beside her and looking at the shape. "What?"

"A carrot!" Dingo said.

Ponto groaned at the bad joke and elbowed Dingo, who croaked a raucous laugh.

Darel sighed. He sometimes wished the Kulipari didn't get bored so easily. He found the cave paintings fascinating.

"Instructions for what?" he asked Yabber.

"That is yet another answer I'm seeking. But why else would King Sergu send me here? And some of

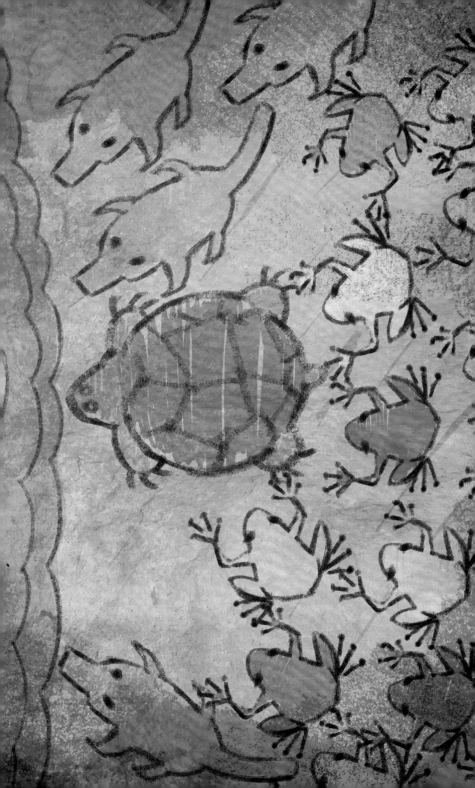

these drawings were made fairly recently. For example . . ." Yabber moved his torch to illuminate a different section of cave wall. "Look at *that*."

Darel gasped when he saw it. A picture, bigger than all the others, of the Rainbow Serpent: a multicolored snake that arched across the sky.

"They say when you see a rainbow," Yabber said in a hushed voice, "it's actually the Serpent, moving from one watering hole to another."

For a long moment, nobody spoke, not even Dingo. They simply gazed at the painting in the flickering torchlight.

"I heard a story once," Quoba finally murmured, "that in the ancient days, before there was any life in the outback, the Rainbow Serpent summoned a thousand frogs to the endless desert. The Serpent tickled the frogs' bellies until they started laughing, and water gushed from them, creating the rivers and watering holes."

Darel smiled. He liked the idea that frogs gave water to help all life in Australia.

"I don't know," Burnu said, with a dubious croak. "I bet the marsupials tell a story about laughing kangaroos making the rivers."

"And the reptiles think it was giggling lizards," Dingo said.

"It doesn't matter," Yabber told them. "The more I look at the drawings, the more certain I am that this is where we'll find our answers. The old king suggested I come here if things looked bleak and . . . and the story on these walls will save the Amphibilands! And possibly bring peace to the outback."

"Yeah, sure," Burnu said. "A bunch of cave paintings will definitely scare off the scorps and spiders."

"The Rainbow Serpent is the key to our victory," Yabber said sharply. "Where do you think your poison comes from? Why do you glow so brightly—so *colorfully*—when you tap your strength? Because you've been touched by the rainbow. It is the Serpent's power that runs not just through dreamcasting but through the Kulipari."

Burnu opened his mouth to reply, then just nodded.

"I never knew that," Ponto said, flicking his inner eyelids thoughtfully.

"I always thought we were just colorful because it looks so *goooood*," Dingo said. "So, the Serpent will help us protect the Amphibilands?"

"There is more at stake than the Amphibilands,"

Yabber said. "The entire outback hangs in the balance. Water is life, and while Marmoo wants every last drop, I suspect Jarrah wants even more. She plans to force a drought upon the land, which will weaken everyone who opposes her. First she'll take over your homeland. Then she'll cloak the outback in nightcast darkness. Perfect for a spider—and deadly for everyone else."

For a moment, nobody spoke. Darel's worst nightmare was that the scorpions and spiders would take over the Amphibilands. But causing a drought, then covering the entire land in twisted, evil magic *after* destroying the Amphibilands? That was even worse.

"So how's the Serpent going to help us?" Burnu asked.

"I don't know." Yabber frowned in frustration. "If only I could understand these drawings!"

"You said that only the platypuses really understand the Rainbow Serpent," Darel said. "Maybe they can help."

"I said that they're the only ones who even *barely* understand," Yabber said. "But you're right. Not even old King Sergu could decipher the signs as well as the Stargazer. We'll have to travel to the river, and ask them to—" He suddenly stretched his neck closer to the wall. "Hmm, I never noticed that before."

"What?" Darel asked.

"Er, well, I mean to say—I think this one is signed."

Darel hopped closer to inspect a scrawl beneath the big picture. Something looked familiar . . . *No! It couldn't be!* He bulged his throat in disbelief, and looked again.

"That—that says 'Apari!'" he sputtered.

"Your *dad*?" Ponto asked, then looked to the others. "Darel's dad?"

"Well," Burnu said, "he *was* the best Kulipari leader of all time . . . until me."

"Your father was here?" Quoba jumped beside Darel. "*He* drew that?"

"I—I—I guess so."

Darel gazed at the signature in awe. So his father had stood here, in this cave, deep inside the mountains? Had been sent here to draw a picture of the ancient water god who could save them all?

He touched the rough rocky wall with his finger pads and gazed at the drawing of the Serpent. In the gloomy cave, the streaks of color seemed to flicker in the torchlight. Some of the curved arcs went too low, almost like the rainbow had roots underground.

Weird.

Well, maybe his father hadn't been such a great artist. Except, no, it looked like he'd done it on purpose. Darel hopped back and forth, inspecting the drawing from various angles, staring at the stencils and sketches and scratches, wondering why his father had added to the ancient drawings. Finally, he just simply sat and thought about it all.

Until he noticed the others gazing at him expectantly. Then he slitted his nostrils in embarrassment. "Oh . . . um. Did someone say something?"

"No," Quoba said. "We're just wondering what you're thinking."

"Not much." He scratched his chin. "Well, over there, it shows the frogs and scorps fighting, right?"

"Right."

"And here's the Serpent that my dad drew. So . . . first there's a battle, and then we come to the Rainbow Serpent. But what does the Rainbow Serpent *do*?" He pointed at the drawing. "Are those pools of water underneath the Serpent? Tunnels? And what's the huge round blob there?"

"It looks like a rock," Quoba said.

"Or a really fat bullfrog," Burnu said.

"It's Ponto after a feast!" Dingo said.

Darel sighed. "I don't know. How is this supposed to help? Our problem is that the Veil is torn, and the scorps and spiders are going to attack again."

"Maybe the Serpent will help fix the Veil," Burnu said.

"This is about more than the Veil," Yabber told them. "This is . . . aimed at a deeper purpose."

Darel frowned at the wall. "And what's this frog doing?"

He tapped a drawing of a brown frog so young that it still had a tail, a stubby, pointy tadpole tail, splashing in the puddle just beneath the Rainbow Serpent.

"That's not a frog," Burnu told him. "That's a grasshopper."

"It's a tadpole," Dingo said.

"Or a cricket," Burnu said.

"It's got a little tail," Dingo said.

"Maybe it's not a tail," Darel said, slowly. "Maybe it's a weapon."

"Whoa!" Burnu said, hopping beside him. "A boomerang!"

"Would you focus?" Quoba snapped. "We all know you'd rather be cracking scorpion carapace than looking at pictures in the Snowy Mountains, but if Yabber thinks these drawings will bring peace to the whole outback, and if Darel's father actually—"

The scampering of dozens of feet interrupted her, and then a mob of mountain possums rushed into the chamber, squeaking and lashing their long pink tails. A few of them raced to Yabber and whispered into his ear.

"We're under attack," Yabber announced, with a gasp. "The spider queen's forces are heading for the cave."

11

D INGO, MOVE!" BURNU CROAKED. "GET to the high ground, and keep them away."

Dingo leaped from the cavern in a blur. "I'll perforate 'em—whatever they are."

"Ponto, help Yabber back to the campfire!" Burnu called. "We can't let ourselves get trapped in a cave."

"I'm on it," Ponto said.

"And Quoba, you scout the . . ." Burnu glanced around the chamber. "Oh."

Darel looked around and realized that Quoba was already gone. Typical.

He waited a second for Burnu to tell *him* what to do, but Burnu had already gone. That was typical, too. It figured that Burnu didn't think an ordinary wood frog could help fight off an attack. Darel hopped through the entrance, then paused, deciding to hang back and guide Yabber through the narrow places while Ponto pushed the turtle from behind.

Earlier, when they'd climbed down to reach the cave paintings, it had seemed to take forever. But now, with Darel's heart pounding off the seconds, the return trip was over before he knew it. He smelled the smoke of the bonfire near where he'd woken up, then burst into the cavern with the stalactites and the pool of slushy water.

But the cavern was empty.

In a flash, he leaped across the smoky cave, past the fire, and through an archway into a huge chamber. The Komodo dragons were standing at the rear of the chamber, chewing on dried meat. Darel shuddered when he saw them eating—he still hadn't gotten used to how they splattered their food with a thick layer of red spit before swallowing it.

But an instant later, his attention snapped to the front of the cavern, where Burnu and Dingo stood. There was a jagged hole that was flooded with sunlight. Darel blinked at the sudden brightness as he realized that the hole was the exit to the outside world; it almost blinded him after the darkness of the cave. A frigid wind wafted in from the cave entrance, and he narrowed his nostrils against the cold. At least the breeze smelled better than the musty air of the caverns.

He hopped over to Burnu and Dingo, who were

staring into the distance, talking in low tones. "What is it?" he asked.

"I don't know—there's nothing in sight." Burnu stared through the opening, scanning the mountains spreading below them in the clear, sunlit day. "And I can suddenly see for miles around us."

"Weird. What happened to the snowstorm?"

"It stopped. There's not a cloud in the sky."

Instead of feeling relieved at the nice weather, Darel felt a nervous knot in his stomach. "Like . . . *magic*? Do you think Jarrah's behind it?"

Burnu nodded. "It doesn't feel natural. Still, I can't see anyone attacking. Maybe those nervous little mountain possums—"

"Wait." Dingo pointed with an arrow. "*There*."

Darel shaded his eyes. Dingo wasn't pointing to the craggy mountainside below them, where mounds of snow scattered the rocks and shrubs . . . she was pointing into the sky. He peered closer and saw tiny black specks floating over the peak of the next mountain.

At first, he thought they were hawks, but they didn't move right.

"No way," Burnu whispered, his breath clouding in the cold air.

Dingo narrowed her eyes. As the squad archer, she had the best eyesight. Especially when she tapped her poison—then she could count the legs on a centipede from a hundred feet away.

"Spiders," she said.

"In the *air*?" Darel said. "Spiders don't fly."

"They 'balloon,'" Burnu told him. "They let out a superlong strand of silk, and the wind carries it up into the sky. Then they float through the air, dangling on the bottom of the silk, and—"

"Those aren't just spiders," Dingo interrupted. "They're . . . they're carrying something."

"Great," Burnu said. "Spiders with luggage."

Darel looked closer and saw what Dingo was talking about. The spiders, which had just been dots a moment before, were being swept rapidly closer by an unnatural wind. As they neared, he saw they were carrying long wriggling dark things in silken nets . . .

"Snakes," Dingo said. "Taipan snakes, with enough poison to kill a croc."

Burnu reacted immediately. He spun to face into the cave and yelled, "Let's go! Taipan snakes—we can't fight them in a cave!"

"We can't leave," Yabber yelled back from the bonfire cavern.

"Did you hear me? They're *taipan* snakes, they're as poisonous as—"

"As Kulipari? You're poison, too!'

"We can barely tap our poison in this cold, we—"

"We need those drawings, Burnu," Yabber said. "I can *feel* how important they are. We cannot let the spider queen destroy them."

"I'd rather not let her destroy *us*."

"They're a message from the divine Rainbow Serpent, drawn in an ancient cave by Darel's father, to guide us through this war. Nothing's more important than understanding them. Not even our lives."

Burnu slitted his nostrils, then sighed. "Well, in that case, we'll fight them here."

"We'll tie their snakey butts into knots," Dingo said. "We'll scare them right out of their snakeskins."

"We need a plan," Darel said.

Burnu nodded. "Everyone back into the bonfire cavern. That's the most defensible spot. Quoba, you hide in here, and after they pass by, drive the dragons at them from behind. Dingo, climb into the stalactites and shoot them from above. Ponto and I will take them on head-to-head."

"What about Yabber?" Ponto asked, as they leaped into the cave with the stalactites and stalagmites.

Burnu glanced toward Yabber. "He and the mud frog will hide."

Darel inflated his throat and drew his dagger. "I'll fight."

"We need you to protect Yabber," Quoba said.

"You want *Darel* to protect Yabber?" Ponto grunted, in surprise. "Against taipan snakes?"

Darel shook his head. "She just wants to keep me out of the fight."

"Not true," Quoba said. "You might not have a Kulipari's poison, but you have a Kulipari's *heart*."

"Fat lot of good that does," Burnu muttered.

Ponto ribbeted loudly. "You've got to admit he's as brave as any of us, Burnu."

"He's braver than I am!" Dingo called, leaping high overhead and grabbing onto a stalactite with her toe pads. "I'm staying up here when the snakes come."

Darel glared at Burnu, then ushered Yabber behind a thicket of stone columns. He took a few deep breaths before scanning the cavern. Quoba was nowhere to be seen, of course, and Dingo was barely visible, lodged between two stalactites on the ceiling. Burnu and Ponto stood in the open, on a hump in the center of the cavern, watching the entrance. Scowling fiercely.

Behind Darel, Yabber chatted to himself about the

cave drawings, though Darel barely heard him. "It all depends on the Rainbow Serpent, but how? What are we supposed to do? Why did the king guide me here? Perhaps even he didn't know what the Serpent wants. Hmm . . . I need to study those drawings. Well! The Kulipari will defeat the snakes, then I'll have all the time I need. How did they get here so fast? Jarrah is growing too powerful. Taipan snakes! Dreadful creatures . . ."

Darel shot his tongue out a few times, to keep it limber. And to keep himself calm. Taipan snakes couldn't tap into their poison like the Kulipari; they didn't glow with an inner light and harness incredible powers. Instead, they just killed you. If one of them bit you, the poison paralyzed you . . . then you died.

They were fast and strong and fierce. And stealthy, Darel suddenly realized, as one of them slithered into the cavern, moving as fast as rainfall and as quiet as snow. Then he caught glimmers of two more flashing into the cave, long ropy snakes with brown and gray scales outlined in black.

"Kulipari!" Burnu bellowed, drawing his boomerangs.

He leaped sideways and tapped his poison in midair, glowing a bright yellow-green in the dimly lit cave. His boomerangs flashed. He landed on a wall and one of the taipans struck at him, but he was already hopping to the opposite wall. His boomerangs missed the snake, sliced through the smoke over the fire, and slammed into four hulking spider archers taking aim from the entryway.

Meanwhile, the other two snakes closed in on Ponto, their serpentine eyes intent over their rounded snouts. One of them coiled to strike, and Ponto started glowing yellow and black.

The snake struck, and Ponto pivoted, shoving the spiky bracer—a thick leather bracelet—on his left wrist into the snake's mouth, then punching with his right. The snake whipped its long body violently, trying to coil itself around Ponto, and the two of them rolled in a furious tangle across the cave floor as three more snakes entered.

Darel gripped his dagger tight and didn't move a toe pad, didn't make a noise—and for once, neither did Yabber.

Burnu caught his boomerangs and somersaulted over the snake attacking him. He hit the floor beside the new snakes, then leaped immediately away and said, "Now!"

"Yoo-hoo!" Dingo called, from the stalactites above. "Here, snaky-snaky-snaky!"

When the taipans looked upward, Dingo started glowing a brilliant orange-red. Her hands blurred as arrows flew from her bow. The taipans' thick scales deflected some of the arrows, but Dingo turned two of the snakes into pincushions before Ponto glowed even brighter and spun in a circle, holding the taipan and whirling around and around. The snake's long body lashed against stalagmites and walls, then slammed into two other snakes and sent them flying.

One of them coiled in the air, writhing wildly, and whipped Dingo from her perch.

"Hey!" she cried, crashing to the floor in a heap. "Keep your snake to yourself!"

Burnu was trading superfast blows with another snake, desperately dodging the murderous fangs, when a green-brown snake with a scarred snout noticed Darel. Its forked tongue flickered as it slithered forward, ten times as long as Darel was tall. Its poison dripped to the floor, turning a patch of lichen black and charred.

"If you've got any dreamcasting that might help," Darel murmured to Yabber, "now's the time."

"Dreamcasting isn't battle magic," Yabber said. "You know that. I mean to say, it's a gentle art, not a— Look out!"

The green-brown snake struck at Darel, and he leaped desperately aside, slashing with his dagger but missing by an arm's length. The snaked hissed—laughing at him—and struck again. Darel ducked behind a rock column and the snake pursued, fast and fierce, coiling its body behind Darel to keep him from running away.

Darel deflected two blows, but then the snake rammed forward with a massive thrust. Darel backpedaled wildly and tripped over a rock.

The snake hissed and loomed over him, fangs dripping. "Tassssssty."

Darel turned his head to avoid a drop of splashing poison.

"Sssssay good-bye," the snake said, and struck.

Darel shot his tongue out, stuck it to a nearby stalagmite, and pulled himself sideways across the floor. The green-brown snake chomped down hard on the rock where Darel had been, and one of its fangs snapped off.

"Good-bye!" Darel said, leaping in a high arc and landing on the snake's head.

He was about to plunge his dagger into the snake's scales when its tail suddenly whipped at him and flung him against the wall.

For a second, he saw double. Two Pontos wrestling with two snakes. Two blurry Burnus fighting beside two blurry Dingos, beating back four more taipans. Two dozen spiders . . . suddenly fleeing from the cave, to the outside.

What were they doing? Why were the spiders running away in the middle of the battle?

His bewilderment vanished a moment after the spiders did—when ten Komodo dragons came thundering into the cavern, with two Quobas riding in front. Then Darel's vision cleared, and he watched Quoba spin her staff in a deadly circle while the dragons chomped with massive jaws as they lumbered through the cavern. The taipans' poison was deadly, but their fangs couldn't pierce the Komodos' scales, and soon the tide of the battle turned.

Ponto hurled his snake upward, where it slammed against the stalactites in the cavern roof before thudding to the floor. Burnu punched a snake in the snout as his boomerangs hurtled through the air and hit the sides of its head. And a dragon stepped on the green–brown taipan's midsection, giving Darel

the chance to finish it off. In a matter of moments, the dragons defeated the final three snakes, and the cavern fell silent except for faint moans and heavy breathing.

"Whew," Dingo said, lowering her bow. "This weather is *not* good for my poison."

Ponto nodded. "Yeah, the cold saps our strength."

"You're just lazy," Burnu said, flopping down on the floor. "I could've taken 'em all with one boomerang tied behind my back."

"Did you see Darel?" Ponto asked. "He took down a taipan *without* poison."

"Beginner's luck," Burnu scoffed.

"What were those spiders doing?" Yabber asked, peering toward the entryway. "Why did they scuttle off like that?"

Quoba frowned. "I'm not sure. I'll check."

As Quoba slipped to the front of the cave, Dingo collected spent arrows and stuffed them in her quiver. "If you find any more of the spider queen's troops, tell them to come back next week. I'm all out of poison."

"Now you know how *I* feel," Darel said.

"I'm proud of you," Ponto said, putting a few toes on Darel's shoulder. "A wood frog holding off a taipans snake? That's like a butterfly fighting off a hawk."

"Who are you calling a butterfly?" Darel said, then winced at a sudden twinge of pain.

"What happened?" Ponto asked, reaching for his bag of herbs. "Are you okay?"

"I think I sprained my tongue."

Ponto snorted and looked around the cavern. "How about the rest of you? Anyone hurt?"

"We're fine," Burnu croaked. "Stop worrying so much."

"No, keep worrying," Quoba said, slipping back into the cavern. "I found the spiders."

"Are they getting ready to attack again?" Ponto asked.

"No, they're scuttling around the mountainside above the cave mouth, weaving a web the size of a eucalyptus tree."

"They chose a weird time to start an art project," Dingo said.

"Whatever they're doing," Quoba said, "it's bad news for us."

"Who cares what they're doing? Let's go kick them in all eight knees," Burnu said. Suddenly, he sprawled onto the ground.

"Burnu!" Darel's called out, his eyes bulging. "Something's wrong with Burnu!"

Ponto leaped across the cavern. He knelt beside Burnu and ran his toe pads over him, frowning at a trickle of blood on his arm. Darel peeked from behind him.

"This is a snakebite," Ponto said. "A taipan got him."

"Just a scratch," Burnu murmured, his head lolling to the side. "I'm fine. Let me at 'em . . ."

"Dingo, get my pack!" Ponto called. "I need more herbs. Yabber, can you help draw out the poison?"

Yabber nodded, his long neck straining forward to look at Burnu's arm. "I'll do what I can."

"Is he going to be okay?" Darel asked, his voice wavering.

"Hmm." Yabber blinked slowly. "Yes. Yes, he is. It's not a deep bite, and he is, after all, a *Kulipari* . . ."

Darel took a shaky breath. "Th-th-that's true."

"Plus, he was tapping his own poison at the time," Yabber said, more confidently. "He'll heal—as long as he doesn't push himself. Well! We must stay here while he recovers and study those drawings."

The turtle half-closed his eyes, and the air thickened around him as he started dreamcasting a healing spell. However, being Yabber, he continued talking at the same time. "Did the spider queen truly think that a surprise attack would keep us from finding the drawings? As if a few taipan could stop the Kulipari! What a foolish plan. I cannot imagine *what* she was thinking . . ."

A sick feeling rose in Darel's stomach as Yabber trailed off. Sending snakes to stop the Kulipari did sound pretty stupid. But Jarrah wasn't dumb. So what was she really up to? Was she planning something else entirely? What if sending the taipan snakes wasn't her only attack? What if that had just been a distraction?

And what exactly were those spiders doing?

While Yabber and Ponto treated Burnu, Darel started for the big cavern with the jagged exit, absently petting his Komodo as he passed.

"Be careful," Quoba said, following him toward the entrance cavern. "There are spiders right outside the cave, higher on the mountain."

"I know," he told her. "And we've got to figure out what they're up to."

The huge cavern glowed with daylight and smelled of a mix of the freezing, fresh air and Komodo poop from where they'd been stabled in the back. With his fingers on his dagger, Darel crept toward the jagged cave opening, flicking his inner eyelids against the brightness.

He cocked his head. "Do . . . do you hear that?"

"Sounds like a snoring dragon," Quoba said.

Darel poked his head through the opening. The cave was high in the mountains, with thick snow above and rough, icy outcroppings below. The cold wind cut into his sensitive amphibian skin, but at least it smelled pure and clean.

A shadow moved below him. He didn't see anything down there, so he figured it must be coming from higher on the mountain, directly overhead. He craned his neck and saw spiders scuttling across the mountainside, over the cave opening. Dozens of long silken threads floated in the air above them, reaching halfway to the clouds, and as he watched, they lifted off one by one, carried into sky by their silk.

They were tugging something up with them. A huge web.

As the ballooning spiders rose higher, the web shifted. Mounds of snow started to spill forward, toward Darel. Just a trickle at first, then faster. What were they doing? Trying to airlift snow to the desert? It would melt before they left the foothills.

Then a whole different kind of chill cut through him.

"Avalanche!" he shouted, as snow started thundering toward the cave. "The spiders are trying to trap us!"

12

WHEN A BURBLE OF RUNNING water sounded through the trees, Gee paused for a moment and cocked his head. "Sounds like a river," he told Coorah.

Coorah nodded. "Must be the platypus village."

"Pippi's going to be pretty happy." He smiled, imagining her excitement. "I bet she'll whack her tail around and smack her bill."

"She's sweet."

"She's nuttier than a macadamia tree," Arabanoo said, jumping down from a branch.

"Look who's talking, sap-sucker," Gee said.

"Mud-belly," Arabanoo answered.

Farther ahead on the forest trail, Pippi turned and called, "C'mon, we're almost there! We're almost home!"

Gee winked his inner eyelid at Arabanoo and Coorah, then hopped beside Pippi. "How can you tell? Is your beak tingling?"

"It's a *bill*!" she said, indignant.

"Oh, right." He nodded thoughtfully. "Because its full name is 'William.'"

"What? That's not its name, that's . . . oh, stop *teasing* me!" She tried to thwack him with her tail, but he leaped away.

Gee laughed, and Pippi laughed along, a funny wheezing giggle. Platypuses—or platypi, or however you said it—were awesome. All furry and beaky and goofy. And Gee and Pippi had become good friends in the past few days, since Chief Olba had called a town meeting.

After everyone had gathered in the hall, the chief had explained that the platypus tribe was in trouble. She'd said that a handful of volunteers should help fight the ghost bats, but they couldn't send too many frogs, in case the scorpions or spiders attacked. She was reluctant to send just a few warriors to face such a great danger, without the Kulipari, so she'd called a chorus—a kind of village vote. The tree frogs peeped and the bullfrogs trumpeted and the Baw Baws rasped. In the end, the frogs who wanted to help the platypus village won the vote.

Chief Olba had asked for volunteers, and Gee had immediately hopped forward. Without even looking, he'd known that Coorah was beside him. And Arabanoo—who had a crush on Coorah—was right there, too, with his squad of white-lipped tree frogs.

"Stay safe," Chief Olba told them. "Try to help the platypuses. And keep in mind that we don't know why the ghost bats are attacking. It's not like them. It doesn't make sense."

"What do you think is happening?" Gee had asked.

"I don't know," she'd said. "But I've got a feeling that Jarrah is involved."

Gee had promised to keep his eyes open, and braced himself for the first obstacle: telling his parents. But they'd taken the news well. His mother gave him her shield from the old days. His father muttered that he blamed Darel for all this warrior nonsense, but they both hugged Gee when he headed through the Veil.

And now he and his friends had almost reached Pippi's village. Gee jumped onto a low branch and saw the river glinting in the evening light. He couldn't wait to get there and see an entire *village* of Pippis! And sure enough, Pippi started charging through the underbrush, moving pretty fast for a fluffy fuzzball who couldn't even hop. A second later, she disappeared down the riverbank and splashed into the water.

"Okipippi!" a happy voice shouted. "Look, it's Pippi! She's okay!"

By the time Gee reached the river, a crowd of excited platypuses had surrounded Pippi, laughing and splashing, and wiping away tears of relief. Gee watched from the shallow water beside the riverbank, a wide grin on his face, until Pippi suddenly said, "Oh! Meet my new friends! The frogs—they saved my life!"

Suddenly, a dozen platypuses swam over to Gee and the other frogs, all talking at once, thanking them and thwacking their tails happily.

Pippi's parents arrived, smiling and crying at the same time, so relieved to find Pippi safe. They kissed and hugged her, and her father scolded her for running away. But when Pippi introduced Gee and the other frogs, her father insisted that the frogs sleep in their burrow during their visit.

"I'll make shrimp burgers and squeeze some fresh larva juice," her father said.

"Oh, we don't want to put you to any trouble," Coorah said, politely.

"Unless you'd prefer something sweet?" Pippi's mother asked. "Honeyed worms?"

"That's very kind," Coorah said, "but we brought food from home, and we—"

"We'd *love* some honeyed worms," Gee cut in, elbowing Coorah. "Honey and worms are two of my favorite things."

"Pippi's back, Pippi's back!" a few platypups called, sliding down the muddy riverbank to splash into the water.

One of the platypuses started to sing in a sweet, chirping voice. A moment later, the others joined in, trilling a watery sort of song and swimming in circles and spirals, diving and splashing in a complex, beautiful river dance.

Pippi sang along, then grabbed Gee as she swam past. "It's a celebration song!" she cried. "Come on, dance and sing!"

"Uh . . . ," he said.

"C'mon!" she urged. "All of you!"

Arabanoo and the white-lipped tree frogs escaped into the tree roots and Coorah stayed with the adults, but Gee laughed and joined in. He ribbeted along with the song as well as he could as he followed Pippi in the crazy platypus dance, swimming underwater while rolling over a few times, then bursting onto the surface to sing some more.

Finally, the celebration ended and all the platypuses tapped Gee with their bills, which was their way

of patting him on the back. They lazed in the river, catching their breath, until one platypus said, "This is the first good news we've had in days."

All the relaxed platypus faces suddenly grew grim.

"What happened?" Pippi asked. "Did something bad happen while I was gone?"

"We managed to fight off the ghost bats that first time," her sister Pirra said. "But they've been coming back every nightfall. They . . . they've got seven of us so far."

"S-s-seven?" Pippi said, and her eyes welled with tears. "Who?"

Gee bowed his head as Pippi and Pirra spoke in low, sad tones. The bats had kept attacking and attacking. They'd killed seven platypuses, and everyone else in the tribe was afraid to leave their burrows after sunset. They were hunting and fishing during the day, but that wasn't natural for them, so they were already running low on food.

As Gee listened, Pippi's father edged near him. "Gurnugan?"

"Yes, sir?" Gee asked.

"Sunset is coming. We should get ready."

"Yeah." Gee looked from the riverbank to the overhanging trees. "First we need to build some defensive fortifications."

"I meant," Pippi's father told him, "we should get inside and hide."

"We're not here to hide, sir. We're here to fight."

"I thought . . . I thought you just came along to see Pippi safely home."

"The frogs voted to help you," Gee told him. "The Kulipari are on a mission, so we came instead. We're like . . ."

"The Uncool-ipari," Arabanoo called, from his perch on a thick tree root.

Gee slitted his nostrils in amusement. "Yeah, but *we* don't need poison to kick bat butt." He turned to Pippi's father, who looked alarmed at Gee's use of the word "butt." "Uh, sorry. Bat bottom? Anyway, what happened after Pippi left?"

"We tried to fight the bats," Pippi's father said sadly. "We've got venom, so we're not defenseless, but they're too quick. And they fly. No platypus can beat a flyer—we can't even get near them."

"*We* can," Gee promised.

Pippi's father looked at each of them in turn, then he shook his head. "You're so young."

"Well, yeah." Gee didn't know what to say. "But, uh . . ."

"Have you heard of Darel?" Coorah asked Pippi's father. "The frog who saved the Amphibilands?"

"Of course," he said.

"Gee has trained with him since they were tadpoles."

Pippi's father cocked his head and looked at Gee. He was clearly impressed. Gee felt embarrassed until Arabanoo nudged him from behind; then he stood a little straighter.

"The two of them survived the scorpion camp," Coorah continued. "They traveled to the Turtle Coves and found the Kulipari. Gee is tougher than he looks. And we *all* fought the scorps and spiders. We may be young, and I can't promise that we'll beat the bats, but we've faced long odds before. And we've won."

For a moment, there was no sound except the gentle burbling of the river and the soft muttering of platypus conversations. Then Pippi's father sighed. "That was the entire Amphibilands, though. Along with the Kulipari and the Turtle King. There aren't even ten of you."

"How many bats are there?" Gee asked.

"A whole swarm. A legion."

One of the white-lipped tree frogs gulped loudly.

Gee managed not to say anything, but he felt a little woozy. A *legion* of ghost bats? He'd expected maybe five or ten, not an entire legion.

"You should talk to the Stargazer," Pippi's father said. "Maybe she can help—she's not a fighter, but she knows this river like the back of her tail."

Gee nodded. "We need all the help we can get."

"She asked to be left alone while she meditates on the Rainbow Serpent, but maybe it's time to check on her." Pippi's father looked over his shoulder and called, "Pippi! Take the frogs to the Stargazer."

Pippi splashed through the water to them. "Sure, Dad."

"And be careful."

She promised she'd come straight back to the burrow, then beckoned to Gee and the others. "C'mon, everyone. The Stargazer lives upstream. She'll know exactly what to do. She knows *everything*."

Most of the tribe's burrows were nestled in a bend where the river was wide and slow, but the waterway narrowed as it rose toward the Stargazer's burrow, and the water moved faster and rougher. As Pippi and the frogs left the village behind, a mist rose around them, like a thick fog. They'd traveled by day—despite Pippi's yawning complaints—to arrive at the village before dusk, when the bats woke. Now the sun was low in the sky, sending orangey rays through the tree-tops.

Gee and Coorah hopped from stone to stone in the river, Pippi swam, and the tree frogs stuck to the roots and branches on the bank. Nobody spoke, probably because they were all thinking about what Pippi's sister had said. Seven platypuses had been killed by the bats . . . and there was no end in sight.

Not unless *they* stopped them. But Gee knew they couldn't defeat a whole swarm of ghost bats in open combat. They just couldn't. They'd have to depend on the Stargazer for a plan.

When the river turned to rapids, the water churning white and furious, Pippi pointed to an over-hanging shrub. "Over there!" she shouted, above the roar of the current. "She lives behind that riberry tree! I'll get her!"

Gee scanned the area as Pippi disappeared behind the roots of the riberry tree. The river sloped upward from the Stargazer's burrow, and whipped into a crazy white froth with dozens of round boulders poking through. Sprays of water splashed Gee as he waited for Pippi, and he "tasted" the fresh water through his skin. The river reminded him of the Amphibilands, and he'd liked every platypus he'd met. Now he just needed to keep them safe. But how were a handful of frogs going to defeat a legion of ghost bats? They couldn't fight them in the air. They didn't even have poison like the platypuses.

As he thought things through, his gaze fell on a huge boulder in the middle of the river, almost entirely hidden by high sprays of water. The rapids slammed the rocks on every side of the boulder, the water shooting into the air like shimmering curtains.

Squinting in the low sunlight, Gee peered closer. Was that an *animal* sitting in the center of the sheets of water?

He bulged his eyes to get a better view, and Pippi stepped from the mouth of the Stargazer's burrow and called, "She's not inside! She's probably—"

"What's that?" Gee interrupted, pointing to the boulder.

"That's *her*!" Pippi yipped, and she leaped into the water. "C'mon!"

Gee glanced at Coorah, then shrugged and followed the young platypus. He jumped from rock to rock as the spray freckled him, and finally he cannon-balled through a curtain of water and landed on the boulder, dripping wet.

A platypus was standing in the center of the boulder. She was small and gray-furred . . . and spinning in circles.

"Um," Gee said. "Hello?"

She didn't seem to hear him. She kept spinning, and her eyes were wide, as if she were watching something fascinating. He got a little dizzy just looking at her.

"I'm Gee," he croaked. "From the Amphibilands."

A dark shape appeared on the other side of the shimmering sheets of water, and then Pippi climbed onto the rock, water dripping from her fur.

"Is . . . is this her?" Gee asked.

Pippi nodded "Oh. Hmm. She's in a trance."

"A trance?"

"She does that," Pippi explained. "She can't hear you until it's over."

"How long will that take?"

"I don't know. A few hours or . . ."

"Or what?"

"Or days. It depends on the rainbows."

"On the *what*?"

"The rainbows," Pippi said, and gestured with her webbed paw. "Once they get her started, it's hard to stop."

Gee looked away from the Stargazer for the first time, and his breath caught. He opened his mouth but couldn't speak. He just stared in amazement.

With the sun slanting low through the trees, hundreds of tiny rainbows shone in the watery curtains that surrounded them. Shimmering rainbows like he sometimes saw in water spray, but brighter and sharper and *everywhere*. They glinted and wavered, and the crashing of the water sounded almost like words, like an impossibly ancient creature was whispering in his ear.

The feeling only lasted a second. Then he blinked and said, "Can't we just shake her?"

"No." Pippi wrinkled her bill. "She's too deep in the trance. If we wake her before she's done, she'll just start hibernating. To recover her strength, I guess."

"She'll fall asleep? Like, immediately?"

Pippi nodded. "In an eyeblink. Deeper than a normal sleep, though. And for a long time."

"So we can't even talk to her?"

"Not now," Pippi said. "Sometimes she'll say things in a trance, but she's hard to understand."

"What kinds of things does she say?"

"Things like . . . 'Blue Sky King.'"

Gee inflated his throat. "That's what she calls Darel?"

"Uh-huh."

"I hope nobody ever tells *him*," Gee said. "I'll never hear the end of it."

"Er . . . but if the Stargazer can't help, I don't see how you can fight off an entire legion of bats."

"Me, neither."

"So what do we do?"

Gee looked at the rainbows. "We fight them anyway."

13

SLABS OF SNOW AND DIRT CRASHED down the mountainside. The noise was deafening, and the ground shook as Darel scrambled to warn the others. "Quoba, get the dragons!" he shouted, leaping into the cavern with the bonfire. "Dingo—tap your poison and drag Burnu outside. Ponto, you help Yabber."

Nobody said anything about him being a wood frog. They just burst into action, moving as fast as only Kulipari could.

Darel grabbed the pack of medicine and turned to head outside as dust and debris started billowing in from the cave entrance . . . and that's when he saw the mountain pygmy possums. A dozen of them, trembling in the corner, big-eyed and terrified.

"C'mon," he yelled at them. "Let's go!"

They trembled some more.

"Oh, great," he muttered, as the avalanche outside

grew even louder. He hopped across the cavern and landed on the other side of the possums. "Shoo!" he yelled, waving his arms. "Run!"

They started scampering for the exit, and he hopped behind them, shouting at them to move faster. In the front cavern, the jagged entrance hole was only a tiny slit of daylight, clogged with dust and debris . . . and closing rapidly. Snow and boulders had almost filled the area, and Darel clambered over the uneven surface, driving the possums in front of him. The opening shrank as he approached, and by the time the last possum had run to safety, it was too narrow for him.

He couldn't fit through. He was about to be buried alive.

A choking dust filled the cavern. The noise was terrible, and he wanted to cry. He'd never get back to the Amphibilands. He'd never see his mother again or the triplets or Gee and Coorah. He'd die in the Snowy Mountains, alone and far from home.

Then a strained voice said, "Anytime you're ready, Darel."

He blinked his inner eyelids and saw a dim yellow-and-black glow. It was Ponto, crammed into the rubble-filled opening, holding Yabber on his shoulders, blocking the debris with Yabber's shell. Ponto was being compressed downward, but there was still a tiny space underneath him, just big enough for Darel to crawl through.

Darel leaped forward, faster than he'd ever leaped before, and he squirmed through the opening under Yabber like a greased polliwog. On the other side of Yabber's shell, the avalanche was like a monsoon pounding down, but Darel just closed his eyes and headed away from the cave. He smashed hard into the wall of falling snow. He heard Ponto grunt behind him, and caught a glimpse of a yellow-and-black blur whizzing past, carrying what looked like a massive umbrella—which was Yabber, who'd drawn himself as deeply into his shell as possible for a turtle with such a long neck.

Then a giant freezing fist of snow punched Darel in the head and flung him upside down. A slab of rock slapped his back, knocking him forward, and he tumbled and gasped, struggling for breath in the maelstrom. He slammed into a boulder that was bounding down the mountainside, and realized that if he didn't break free of the avalanche, he'd get crushed into frog jelly.

But he was so dizzy that he couldn't even tell which

way was up. And being suffocated in snow chilled him to the core—he felt himself getting sleepy, despite the terrified pounding of his heart. He flipped and flopped downward, like one of his little sister's stuffed animals going over a waterfall.

Then something grabbed his left foot. Something strong and ropy.

A second later, he was jerked from the crashing avalanche and lifted high into the air. He croaked in relief as he dangled by his toe pads, watching snow and dirt pour down the mountain like a raging river.

His pulse still racing, he swayed wildly in the wind kicked up by the avalanche. He peered upward, half expecting that Dingo had tied a rope to an arrow and lassoed him.

Instead, he saw Quoba above him, with her mouth open and her tongue stretched out in a long pink line, sticking to his foot. Above her, he caught a glimpse of Dingo, *her* tongue fully extended, attached to Quoba's arm. Dingo held onto the scaly tail of her Komodo, its body wedged into a craggy outcropping. With a great deal of mumbling and bouncing around, they dragged Darel to safety above the cave opening.

Well, above where the opening *used* to be. Because

it was gone. Buried under tons of snow and rocks.

Quoba must've seen his face. "The cave's gone," she told him, rubbing her jaw. "We're lucky to be alive."

"The *drawings* are gone." Darel groaned. "My father's drawings. Yabber said we need them to bring peace to the outback."

"Maybe he's wrong," Quoba said. "We don't know that for sure."

"And now we never will."

Darel inflated his throat in despair, then flopped onto his back on the cold, hard ground beside the big Komodos, staring at the sky. His body ached, and his mind felt empty and hopeless. He *did* know that those pictures were the key to victory. Why else would his father have drawn on a cave wall? Why else would King Sergu have suggested that Yabber come to this cave?

He gazed at the dark clouds, which had been gathering since the spider queen had stopped messing with the weather. Looked like rain. Great. That was all they needed.

He lay there a long time, absently stroking his Komodo's tail. The big lizard turned after a while and gave him a lick with a tongue as raspy as an ironbark tree.

As the first droplets of rain started to fall, Darel looked to the other end of the outcropping, where Ponto and Yabber were crouched over Burnu. Ponto was applying some sort of paste to the taipan bite, while Yabber was swaying slightly, his eyes closed.

"How is he?" Darel called as the rain pitter-pattered off the Komodos' scales.

"Weak," Ponto told him.

"Am not," Burnu slurred. "I'm just a little cold."

"We're *all* cold," Dingo said. "And I'm tapped out. I need rest before I use my poison again."

"Me, too," Ponto said.

"At least we've still got Quoba," Darel said.

"That's right." Quoba smiled. "I'll keep you all safe. Lazy tadpoles."

"Safe from what?" Dingo asked, opening her mouth to let the drizzle fall on her sore tongue. "We defeated the snakes, the spiders ballooned away—"

"And we still lost," Darel said. "We lost the cave. We lost the drawings."

"So what do we do?"

"We carry on," Yabber said, turning his head

toward them. "You wanted to bring me back to the Amphibilands, so that's where we'll go."

Darel nodded, inflating his throat sadly as he watched the tiny specks of the ballooning spiders float toward the desert. A faint blur around the spiders made him think they were being attacked by mosquitoes or wasps, but even that didn't cheer him up. They'd lost the drawings, they'd lost the cave. And Darel worried that they'd lost the war.

14

WHEN THE SWARM OF GHOST BATS appeared through the trees, Gee tightened his grip on the leaf-ball in his hand. But other than that, he stood as still as a statue.

Along with Coorah and eight of the bigger platypuses, he waited on a flat rock in the shallows of the river. As he watched the bats flitting closer, he felt the weight of the ball in his hand. It was heavier than it looked, a bunch of leaves tightly wrapped around a mess of goop.

"You think these things are going to work?" he asked Coorah.

"Of course!" She slitted her nostrils. "Maybe. Er . . . I've got no idea."

"Well, it's worth a try."

As wisps of white darted and dipped in the darkness, Gee hung the leaf-ball from his belt and drew his wooden club. He counted five bats, then ten . . . then he stopped counting. There were at least twenty of them. He inflated his throat to give himself courage as the platypuses around him all shifted onto three legs, so they could use the venomous spur they each had on one ankle.

The bats swarmed closer until a white cloud hovered high above the river, staying out of range of the frogs' tongues.

"Oooh, frogs," one of them hissed. "*I love frogs. So tasty.*"

"*And I'm hungry,*" another hissed. "*Spending too much time here, not enough time hunting. We can't even eat platypuses. Frogs, on the other paw, are delicious . . .*"

"Hey, batbrain," Gee croaked. "I've swallowed *flies* bigger than you."

When the ghost bat swooped at him, Gee shot out his tongue.

The bat somersaulted away, dodging Gee's tongue, and whispered, "*You're too slow!*"

Then a pebble smacked into one of its wings. The bat veered wildly through the air, hissing, and crashed into the muddy bank.

"One down," Coorah said, putting another pebble into her slingshot.

"Nineteen to go," Gee said. "Hey! Come and get it, ghosties!"

As one, the swarm of bats dived toward the flat rock, like white streaks in the gloom. They dove and rolled in the air, and whenever a platypus swiped with a spur, the bat danced away and another bat swiped down with fangs flashing. Gee leaped into the air and smashed one with his club, then got knocked sprawling by another bat's wing. He landed beside Coorah, who looked a little shaky after having her leg slashed by a fang.

"Now?" she asked Gee.

"Not yet," he said, jumping and slamming into a bat that was about to sink its teeth into a furry platypus's neck. He hopped up and down on the bat a few times, then shouted, "Is that all you've got? You're not bats—you're rats! You're not ghosts—you're toast! You're—"

The entire swarm of bats wheeled in the air and shot directly at Gee, hissing and flapping in a fury.

"Now!" he shouted, leaping backward. "Now, now, *now*!"

Arabanoo and his tree frogs burst from the leaves all around. Each of them leaped at a bat, held tight with tree-frog toe pads, and cannonballed into the river. Water splashed everywhere, and in an instant, half the bats were submerged.

The rest paused in the air, and that's when Gee

threw his leaf-ball. He hit a scowling bat right in the chest, and the leaf-ball burst open. Pepperbush goop splattered through the air, and the bats started screaming and rising higher above the river.

"It burns!" one hissed. *"It burns!"*

"Get back down there," another said, whacking the first bat with his wing. *"Or Queen Jarrah will show you what hurt is."* And that's when Coorah sent her last pebble arcing through the air with her slingshot. She hit a wasp's nest that was dangling in the highest reaches of a river tree. For a moment nothing happened . . . Then the air started writhing with angry wasps and shrieking bats. The white wisps sped away, with the vicious wasps trailing behind them, leaving the village in peace.

"Whew," Gee said, rubbing his bruised elbow. "That was close."

"I'm just glad they retreated." Coorah hopped toward an injured platypus, taking a bandage from her pouch. "I'm all out of pepperbush goop."

"It finally worked, though."

"I think it scared them more than anything."

"That's okay, they scared *me* more than anything."

"Yeah. And I don't think that was even an entire legion of bats. We got lucky, this time."

"What did you say to make them charge?" Arabanoo asked Gee, emerging from the river. "'You're not ghouls—you're fools?'"

"No, I said—" Gee caught a glimpse of motion in the distance, and gasped. "Oh, no. That *wasn't* an entire legion . . ."

Dozens of white wisps were flitting through the dark forest toward them. Twice as many as before. And Gee didn't have any defenses ready: no frogs in the trees, no pepperbush goop.

"Run!" he shouted. "Back to the burrows, now!"

15

STANDING BESIDE LORD MARMOO, PIGO peered with his main eyes toward the distant peaks of the Snowy Mountains. They'd arrived hours earlier, marching alongside the spider queen, who'd been carried on a covered platform strewn with fragrant pink petals. Jarrah had remained inside as the sun burned down, but her ladies-in-waiting shifted and grumbled in the bright heat.

Pigo excused himself from Lord Marmoo, edged closer to the ladies-in-waiting, and stood quietly. Might as well try to eavesdrop on the spiders. Otherwise, he was just wasting time. Thirty spiders and ten scorpion soldiers were all waiting for Jarrah to plan her next move. Plus, the spider queen was making Lord Marmoo wait, which angered Pigo, though he managed not to show it. No, better to appear calm as he tried to learn everything he could about the process that would harden his lordship's carapace.

After a time, one of the ladies-in-waiting nodded

to him. "Commander Pigo," she murmured in greeting.

"A fine day," he said. "Though maybe a little warm for spiders."

"Perhaps a trifle," she said.

"We like the heat. But we believe in always being prepared." He nodded to two of his scorpion warriors, who'd brought a tent for Marmoo. "Would you like a little shade?"

"Very much!" she said.

Pigo had the warriors erect the tent, then stood in the open flap as the ladies-in-waiting clustered in the shaded interior. They cooled their faces with silken fans and started gossiping among themselves. Pigo nodded along, and every now and then asked a question about the queen's powers and plans.

"Queen Jarrah invented nightcasting," one of the ladies told him. "She's been training us since she, uh . . . *lost* her previous apprentices."

He nodded as he edged inside the tent. He knew all about how Yabber defeated the previous ladies-in-waiting. "But she's stronger now," he said.

"Much stronger. Her poison is twice as powerful, and her webs are twice as sticky."

"And . . . are those the webs that will harden Lord Marmoo's carapace?"

The lady nodded. "Only Jarrah's webs can hasten your lord's transformation."

"Yet Her Majesty seems reluctant to do so," Pigo said lightly, hoping to discover the real reason Jarrah kept delaying.

"Once Lord Marmoo's carapace has toughened," the lady murmured, leaning closer, "*nobody* will be able to stand against him. Not even Queen Jarrah. Perhaps she's simply waiting to make sure he'll remain loyal to her."

"She should have no fear on that account," Pigo lied.

"I hope you're right." The spider fluttered her fan. "Now, tell me a little about—"

A sudden buzzing filled the air, and Pigo sprang from the tent and tracked motion with his side eyes, a messy blue-tinted cloud that grew denser at the edge of the plateau. He spun quickly, his tail cocked and his pincers tensed, ready to pounce if the cloud proved dangerous.

A silken laugh rang out from the spider queen's platform. "Put your weapons away. These are friends—my new friends, the blue-banded bees."

Jarrah slunk onto the hard rock of the plateau, and the cloud—the swarm of bees—shifted toward her.

There must've been hundreds of them, with trans-
lucent wings and tiny stingers and bright blue bands
around their abdomens.

The bee-cloud seemed to bow to Jarrah. All of
them, speaking in a single buzz said, "We did as you
commanded us, Your Majesty."

"Of course you did," she purred. "If you hadn't,
I'd cut off your water once I control the springs of the
outback. All your hives withered, all your brood dead.
Now, tell me what you learned."

"We flew into the mountains," the buzz said. "We
met your spiders, floating from strings—"

"Ballooning," she corrected.

"Ballooning so slowly," the bees buzzed, and Pigo wondered if he was only imagining scorn in the noise. "From strings."

Pigo worked his mouthparts curiously. Clearly, the bees only obeyed Jarrah because they knew the Amphibilands would fall eventually, and Jarrah and Marmoo would control the biggest source of water in the outback.

"We asked your spiders what happened," the buzz continued, "as you commanded us. Ballooning so slowly. They'll arrive sooner or later, but without wings they drift like puffs of pollen—"

"Enough!" Jarrah said. "What did they *say*?"

"The taipan snakes entered the cave, and your spiders heard fighting. They arranged the web as ordered, and dragged it across the mountainside."

"And did it work? Did they start an avalanche?"

"Yes, Your Majesty." The tight cloud of bees seemed to bow. "They said the mountain fell like a rotten tree."

"Excellent," Jarrah purred. "And then?"

"And then a pillar of dust rose as the entire mountainside collapsed."

"And the turtle?" she asked, eagerly. "He was crushed?"

"No," the buzz said. "The frogs dragged him to safety."

"*What?*" Jarrah shrieked. "He survived?"

"Yes, Your Majesty. He—"

In a flash, she drew a strand of silk from her spinnerets and flicked it through the air. It *cracked* like a whip, scattering the bees and sending Jarrah's cushioned platform flying. As the sound echoed over the desert, Pigo felt himself blasted backward by a burst of nightcasting power. He gritted his mouthparts and kept the fear from his face.

When the echo faded, Jarrah spoke. "I've summoned my special troops."

"You're sending them after the frogs?" Marmoo asked.

"And the turtle," she said.

"Harden my carapace, and I'll join them. I'll bring you Yabber's shell."

She ran the silken thread between her fingers. "No. I'll go myself."

"Why do you care about the dreamcaster?" Marmoo asked. "We already tore a hole in the Veil. We can seize the Amphibilands with one sudden attack."

"Killing the croakers isn't my goal, Marmoo. I

dream bigger than you. Why stop with the Amphibi-lands?"

"Because it contains all the water we'll ever need."

"Ah, but you're the one who thirsts for water. I thirst to prove that nightcasting will *crush* dream-casting. Once I stop that long-neck turtle and the Rainbow Serpent, the entire outback will bow to my nightcast will."

Pigo frowned to himself. So Queen Jarrah didn't care about water; she cared only about magic? That made her even more unpredictable . . . and dangerous.

But Marmoo merely nodded. "You told me that the Rainbow Serpent is the source of dreamcasting. So you'll stop the turtle from joining forces with it?"

"The Serpent doesn't join forces. It merely speaks, and is obeyed or ignored. I'm going to keep the turtle, and his Kulipari puppets, from obeying." She peered at the bees, now less of a tight cloud than a loose swarm. "You, bees!"

"Yessss, Your Majesty?" the bees buzzed, collecting together in front of the spider queen.

"Return to the Snowy Mountains. Find the turtle and his croaker friends. Your job is to slow them down. Once I arrive with my devils, they won't stand a chance."

16

DAREL HELPED PONTO STRAP A moaning Burnu onto the saddle of a Komodo dragon, then clambered onto his own dragon. He arranged the warm rocks from the new fire around him and petted the big beast's scales as he watched Ponto leap up to sit behind Burnu.

"I can hold the reins myself," Burnu grumbled, weakly.

"Sure you can," Darel whispered. "But we've got no other way to convince Ponto to ride a dragon."

"Silly Ponto," Burnu said, handing over the reins.

Ponto frowned. "Riding dragons . . . ," he muttered.

"They're just like crocs," Dingo called back, from farther ahead on the snowy mountain path.

"They're nothing like crocs!"

"Well, they're big and scaly," Darel said, nudging his Komodo onward. "With way too many teeth."

"For generations, we've used crocs as mounts,"

Ponto said. "But Komodo dragons? I don't trust this newfangled stuff."

"New-*fang*led!" Dingo cried. "Ha! Get it?"

Ponto threw a chunk of ice at her head, but she dodged it and urged her mount onward.

A cold, damp wind rose from the valley behind them, and a misty rain speckled Darel's dragon. He tugged gently on the reins, telling his mount to follow Quoba toward a rocky peak. When he reached the top, the mountains spread around him, capped with snow and dotted with trees and bushes. He peered into the distance, where beyond the mist and the endless outback, the Amphibilands waited.

Darel smiled as he thought of the leaf villages and the chief's house and his mother's shop. Safe behind the protection of the Veil . . . as long as the defenses held in the Outback Hills, where the Veil was torn. But what would happen now? Even Yabber didn't know what to do next. They'd come to the mountains to find Yabber, and they'd found him. Yet they'd still failed. They'd lost his father's cave drawings that explained what the Rainbow Serpent wanted them to do.

Still, the rolling motion of Darel's dragon

soothed him as they headed from the peak toward a mountain pass. They bade farewell to the mountain pygmy possums, who scampered around for a while, then disappeared into the bushes.

As they were riding away, Dingo suddenly asked Ponto, "Hey! What does a frog with long ears say?"

"I don't care," he grumbled.

"C'mon! What does a long-eared frog say?"

"There are no long-eared frogs."

"You mean you give up?"

"Fine, I give up. What does a frog with long ears say?"

"'Rabbit!'"

Ponto groaned. "That's awful."

"You're just grumpy because we're big fat losers."

"We're not big fat losers."

"We lost an entire cave, Ponto. We are the *definition* of losers."

"Well, at least we're bringing Yabber back."

"The scorpion lord's planning to tear down the Veil and destroy the Amphibilands, right? And Yabber said the spider queen's trying to destroy the entire *outback*. The whole reason we need Yabber is to defeat them—and he says those cave drawings were going to tell us how. But now? Now we're heading back to the Amphibilands with nothing."

"You know what?" Ponto glared into the distance. "Even your jokes are better than the truth."

"Things aren't so bad," Quoba said. "We beat the snakes—we escaped the cave. We *survived*. And Burnu will recover."

Yabber sighed. "In time."

"Wait a second," Darel said.

"In how much time?" Dingo asked, ignoring him. "It's one little snakebite."

"One little *taipan* bite," Ponto said. "That poison could drop a river shark."

"Hold up," Darel said.

"So we have to drag Burnu's skinny green butt all the way home?" Dingo asked.

"We're not going home," Darel said, speaking more loudly.

Dingo cocked her head. "What? We're not?"

"Not yet," he said.

They all turned to him, and he pointed into the distance.

There, rising above the rest of the mountains, was the tallest peak of all. Targangil, the tabletop moun-

tain. And where the sun sloped through the drizzle, a glorious rainbow fell from the clouds, a bright stripe of red that shaded into yellow and then a blue-green band with a thin purple edge. It shimmered as if it was slithering through the gray clouds, then touched down on top of Targangil.

"First," Darel said, "we're going *there*. To find the Rainbow Serpent."

17

"BACK TO YOUR BURROWS!" GEE shouted again.

"Go!" Coorah yelled at the platypuses, who were frozen at the sight of so many ghost bats. She hopped up and down on the flat rock. "Run! Go!"

The platypuses finally moved. They rushed toward the water, and the few in front slipped into the river before the legion of bats struck. Gee saw one bat slashing at a slower platypus, and he jumped forward to help, but another bat swooped down and chomped on his leg. Gee grunted in pain, then smashed the bat with his club just as a third rammed him. He heard shouts and fighting all around but couldn't see anything clearly as he battled his way through the bats toward the water.

At the very edge of the flat rock, he stood back to back to back with Coorah and Arabanoo, legs kicking and tongues flashing. They barely held off the onslaught as the last of the platypuses and tree frogs slid and jumped into the river. And then, bleeding and bruised, they too dove underwater.

Gee swam to the opposite bank, his bulging eyes tracking the white blurs that were barely visible flying above the river. He spun underwater, and waved to catch everyone's attention. When they were all looking at him, he counted with his fingers: one, two . . . *three*!

All the frogs and platypuses burst from the water at once, racing for the safety of the burrows behind the overhanging roots. Gee stayed in the water for an extra few seconds, to make sure everyone made it. When he was alone in the water, he swam deeper, braced his webbed feet against the river bottom. He blocked out the throb of pain in his leg and focused.

Then he launched upward, using all the strength in his good leg, and rocketed from the river. He clubbed a bat in the face, landed on the riverbank, kicked another bat, and leaped through the roots into Pippi's burrow.

He collapsed inside, bruised and breathless.

"You're bleeding," Pippi's sister said, helping him deeper into the burrow. "How bad is it?"

"I'm okay." He limped a few steps and almost fell. "Well, maybe a little woozy."

He held himself upright on a burlwood stool, and looked around the chamber. It must've been a warm

and comfy living room once, but now all the furniture had been pushed to the walls. In the center, injured platypuses and frogs were lying on makeshift nest-cots. Pippi's sister led Gee to one and started slathering platypus medicine on his cuts.

One of the injured platypuses started moaning, and Gee felt ashamed. He slumped his shoulders, afraid that everyone was looking at him, blaming him for their defeat. He didn't know what to do, though. He didn't know what to say. He wished Darel were here.

After a minute, Pippi's father clasped his shoulder. "Nobody could've done better, Gurnugan. You did a good job out there."

The halfhearted praise made Gee feel even worse. The platypus tribe had trusted him, and he'd lost the fight. And as the moaning quieted, he realized that the bats were roosting in the roots just outside the burrows, whispering insults and threats.

"... *you can't hide forever,*" one whispered.

"*Stick out your bills and we'll bite them off,*" another said.

"*You're too dumb-looking to live.*"

"*We'll get you all in the end. You know we will.*"

Gee frowned toward the burrow entrance. "What are they doing out there?"

"That's what they do every night," Pippi's sister told him. "They perch on the roots until morning and try to scare us."

"But—but why?"

"I don't know. To keep us in here, I guess."

Pippi's mother bustled from the kitchen, with a tray of snacks. "What you all need is a bite to eat. You fought very bravely, and you whipped that first group of bats, too! I cheered when you young tree frogs jumped out of the trees."

She waddled around the burrow, and the gloom lifted a bit as everyone ate. Gee grabbed a bunch of honeyed worms, which were a thousand times stickier than he was used to—but delicious. "Veeve arr ununvul!" he said.

"Is that the ancient frog language?" Pippi asked.

"No," Coorah said. "He's just talking with his mouth full."

Gee licked his lips. "I said, 'These are wonderful.' They're sticky like glue, though. Your honey is stickier than ours."

"Toss me one," Arabanoo said.

Gee threw one into the air, and Arabanoo shot out his tongue. He caught the honeyed worm and sucked it into his mouth, and the platypuses gasped in surprise, then clapped like it was a trick. Gee threw another worm, but that one stuck to his toe pads, and Pippi laughed, and everyone relaxed for a minute.

Until the whispers of the bats outside slipped into the burrow: *"We'll eat the frogs first, then we'll skin the platypuses."*

"All that lovely fur . . ."

"We'll make hats," another one whispered. *"Big fuzzy hats."*

One of the platypups sniffled. "I don't want to be a hat."

"Don't worry," Coorah told him. "They can't get us in here."

"We don't need to get in there," a bat whispered.

"They can hear us?" Arabanoo asked, his eyes bulging.

"Every word," a bat whispered. *"Have you seen our ears?"*

"We'll starve you out sooner or later," the first bat said. *"You can't hunt while we're here. First you'll get hungry, then you'll get sloppy. Then we'll destroy your entire tribe."*

The platypup started crying, and Pippi gave him a hug and murmured that everything would be okay, but Gee saw that the others looked worried, too. The platypus tribe foraged at night, and with the bats lurking on the roots from dusk until dawn, they'd soon run out of any stored food.

"We'll beat them," Gee said. "I don't know how, but we will."

He opened his mouth to eat another handful of honeyed worms, then paused. He shouldn't eat so much, not now—not with the tribe going hungry.

He tried to put the worms back in the bowl, but they stuck to his toe pads. He picked and pulled at them, which just made his other hand sticky, too. It was like he'd shoved his arms elbow-deep into a vat of glue.

Pippi giggled at him and he grumbled. "This stuff is stickier than tree sap. I'm like a mosquito stuck in fly paper or . . ."

"Or what?" she asked.

Gee didn't answer. He narrowed his nostrils thoughtfully, then looked toward the entrance of the burrow. Very slowly, he inflated his throat in satisfaction. He knew how to fight the bats. He knew how to *win*.

18

FREEZING WIND LASHED ACROSS the Snowy Mountains, but Darel didn't mind the cold. Not anymore. Since seeing the rainbow, he hadn't even felt sleepy.

He swayed in the saddle as his Komodo lumbered through yet another mountain pass, resting but alert. They'd reach the peak of Targangil tomorrow.

When the sky had cleared, the rainbow had faded away, but Darel still saw all the colors every time he closed his eyes. He knew that's where they needed to go. He didn't know *why*, though.

He prodded his Komodo forward, and the great beast scrambled over icy rocks, moving closer to Yabber.

"Yabber," Darel started, then he stopped.

Yabber was asleep in his saddle, his neck curved low over his Komodo's back.

Darel murmured, "Well, I'm glad someone can relax."

"I'm not sleeping," Yabber said, his eyes still closed. "Hardly even dozing."

"Oh! I'm sorry. Were you dreamcasting?"

"I still am."

Darel flicked his inner eyelids, looking closer. Before he'd left the Amphibilands and met the turtles, he'd imagined that dreamcasting would look amazing, with flashing lights and crashing noises. But now that he'd fought and traveled with both King Sergu and Yabber, he still couldn't tell the difference between dreamcasting and napping.

"Looks like snoozing," he said.

"Dreamcasting is a gentle art," Yabber told him. "Excellent for hiding things away, for understanding patterns and predicting the weather . . . but not a very good weapon."

"Unlike nightcasting," Darel said.

Yabber opened his eyes. "Yes, all the spider queen's strength is on the battlefield."

"You did pretty well on the battlefield last time."

"I lost my temper."

"Is that what you call it when you explode with

magical force?" Darel asked. "You blew a dozen scorps halfway across the battlefield."

A hint of a smile curved at Yabber's mouth. "Quite disgraceful. And not something I can do on purpose. If it comes to another fight, I hope I'll find a different way."

"Like what?"

"Well, the Veil keeps our enemies from finding the Amphibilands, right?"

"Right."

"Imagine a Veil that covered just a single warrior, a small one-frog Veil that I could wrap around, say, Dingo."

Darel inflated his throat. "And make her invisible? Like a . . . a cloak!"

"A cloak, yes," Yabber said, and chortled. "A cloaker for a croaker!"

"Your jokes are as bad as Dingo's," Darel groaned. "Can you really do that?"

"Well, no."

"Oh."

"Not yet, at least. I'm still working on my weather control. Getting quite good, if I say so myself."

Darel gestured to the freezing mountain. "You can control the weather? Then make it *warm*!"

"If I warmed the air, the snow would melt—the whole place would flood." Yabber sighed. "Still, I wish I could do something *useful*. Perhaps we won't need any help, after we reach the top of Targangil."

They rode in silence for a minute. "So you think I'm right?" Darel asked. "About going there?"

"I know you are," Yabber said. "The Rainbow Serpent is waiting."

"Do—do you really think so?" He'd told the others they were going to see the Serpent, but he hadn't been sure he believed it himself. "Truly?"

"These days, the only one who heeds the Rainbow Serpent is the Stargazer, but your father must have spoken to it. Or at least listened to it, before drawing those pictures. And I believe that now *we* have been called to Targangil, to receive the Serpent's guidance."

Darel looked toward the peak, which was fading as night fell. "I hope it helps."

From up ahead, Quoba called, "Time to make camp!"

She dismounted in the shelter of a rock outcropping and started building a fire. Ponto found the warmest spot and settled Burnu on a blanket; then he and Yabber checked the snakebite. Darel fed and watered the dragons as Dingo bounded to the top of the rock to take the first watch. Darel turned away as the dragons covered their meat in red spit, and crossed to the warmth of the fire.

Burnu still looked a little faded, but he opened one eye halfway and said, "Are we there yet?"

"Not till tomorrow morning," Ponto said.

"We'll get there early," Quoba said, watching the flames. "And if all goes well, we'll start back to the Amphibilands after . . . whatever happens." She inflated her throat meditatively. "What do we *think* is going to happen?"

"We think the Rainbow Serpent is going to appear to us," Darel told her. "Maybe tell us something. Help us."

"Now we're chasing rainbows?" Ponto grumbled. "The Serpent doesn't talk to anyone who isn't furry with a beak."

"Darel's father wasn't a platypus," Yabber reminded him.

Dingo fell from the darkness above, and landed beside the fire. "We've got company."

Quoba grabbed her staff. "Spiders?"

"I don't think so. It's something weird. I couldn't see exactly, but it looked like—"

"Bees!" Darel shouted, drawing his dagger when he spotted a shimmering cloud in the night.

"This time of day?" Yabber said. "That's not normal."

Ponto eyed the shifting swarm of bees diving toward them. "Jarrah must've sent them."

"We are Her Majesty's loyal subjects," the bees buzzed, and swooped in to attack.

19

AREL LIFTED HIS DAGGER AND crouched, ready to fight. His heart was pounding. Quoba and Dingo flanked him, their weapons drawn.

"Uh," Darel said. "Yum?"

"Yum?" Quoba asked.

Darel flicked out his tongue and caught a bee. He sucked it back into his mouth and swallowed. "Tasty!"

Quoba swatted a bee with her staff, and Dingo swiped it from the air with her tongue. "He's right! Crunchy on the outside, with gooey goodness in the middle."

A bee stung Darel's leg, and he grimaced and shot his tongue out again, catching the bee. He heard Ponto say, "Ow! Ouch! Yum!" and Quoba's tongue flicked past his face and stuck to a bee that was about to sting his neck.

He leaped high to avoid the thick of the swarm, then shot his tongue behind him, swooping up three

more bees. Dingo was zigzagging around, stuffing her face, while Quoba quietly ate her fill and Ponto swiped dozens of the little buzzers from the air with one flick of his tongue. The occasional sting wasn't too bad, considering that an entire buffet had just appeared out of nowhere. They'd been living on dried flies for too long, so they croaked happily, dodging stingers and gobbling the sparkly blue bees.

"Grab some for Burnu and Yabber," Darel said.

"Already on it," Dingo told him, somersaulting past.

Darel hopped and spun and ate—and occasionally yelped at a sting. For a few minutes, he forgot all about the threat to the Amphibilands. He forgot about Marmoo and Jarrah and the Rainbow Serpent. He gorged himself until his stomach bulged.

The remaining bees buzzed louder and louder and seemed to surround Darel and the others in one crazed final assault. Slowed from the feast and aching from the beestings, Darel didn't notice the bees' *real* plan until it was too late.

Then a rumbling caught his attention.

A hissing and stamping from the shadows at the edge of the campfire: the Komodos. Dozens of bees had burrowed under the big lizards' scales, waited for the sign . . . then all stung at once.

The dragons whipped their tails and arched their necks, trying to bite at the tiny bees. When one of them roared and started jolting down the path, it turned into a stampede. All five Komodo dragons thundered down the mountain in a frenzy, their claws scratching over rocks.

"The dragons!" Darel yelled. "They're *goorp—*"

He swallowed the bee that flew directly into his mouth.

"They're running away!" Quoba said, twirling her staff to fend off some bees. "They must've been stung."

Darel crouched to leap after the dragons, but the bees massed in front of him, like a huge stinging wall.

Ponto grunted, jumping high and cannonballing through the bees.

Dingo followed a moment later; then Quoba arced through the air. Darel glanced back at Yabber, to make sure that he and Burnu were safe.

"I'll watch Burnu!" Yabber told him, arching his long neck. "You get the dragons!"

Darel crouched down to jump, but high in the air, the bees had an advantage. They swarmed the Kulipari from all sides, sticking to them like burrs to a bandicoot's butt. Ponto swatted angrily, and Dingo yelped and spun. Quoba simply slitted her nostrils. And when the frogs landed, the bees clung to them, stinging and buzzing. Too many to fight, too many to eat.

"Jump into the snowbank!" Darel yelled. "They make *us* look warm-blooded!"

Dingo said, "Huh?"

"The snowbank!" Ponto said, leaping past.

Quoba didn't say anything. She just dove into the snow and rolled around.

Darel hopped over and used the blunt edge of his

dagger to scrape snow-stunned bees off the others, but by the time he finished, the dragons were long gone, still stampeding through the mountains, some- where, harried by beestings. Too far away to catch.

"That's what they wanted all along," Darel said, looking into the darkness. "To chase off the dragons."

"Why?" Quoba asked.

"Jarrah must want to slow us down." He flicked his inner eyelids. "I don't know why."

"She's probably sending more snakes after us," Dingo said. "And wants to catch us in the cold moun- tains, where we're weaker."

"Well, if she was trying to slow us down, she suc- ceeded," Ponto said, rubbing at the beesting lumps on his head. "Without the dragons, we *won't* get there tomorrow morning."

20

EE SQUATTED BESIDE PIPPI ON THE Stargazer's rock. Sheets of water fell all around them. There were even more rainbows than before, and the Stargazer seemed deeper in her trance, humming to herself as she spun in slow circles. Her dark eyes flicked, and occasionally a soft smile curved her bill, but she didn't even seem to notice that she wasn't alone.

The water gurgled and murmured, and for a second Gee imagined that the splashing sounded like words. Then it just sounded like splashing again. Nobody was saying anything.

"Looks like she's not waking up anytime soon," Gee said with a sigh.

"I've never seen her like this for so long." Pippi touched one of the walls of water, and it parted for her paw. "I've never seen half so many rainbows, either."

"What does it mean?"

"I don't know. I guess the Serpent is more active than usual."

Gee inflated his throat thoughtfully. "Well, one thing is clear. We can't expect the Stargazer to help us tonight."

"She doesn't know anything about fighting, any-way."

"We'll go ahead with my plan, then."

Pippi eyed him. "Your plan is crazy."

"Crazy like a frog," he said.

"What does that mean?" She cocked her head. "Is that a saying? 'Crazy like a frog'?"

"It is now."

"You're weird."

"That's why you two are friends," Arabanoo said, hopping through the sheet of water. "C'mon, Gee. Time to get ready."

Pippi's bill curved in a smile that made Gee smile in return. He knew that she liked being friends—and thought that she even liked being "weird" together.

Then the young platypus told the Stargazer, still in her trance, "I don't know if you can hear me, but I should go with them. I'll come back when I can."

The gray-furred Stargazer swayed slowly, peering at the rainbows. Pippi left some food at the old platypus's feet; then they splashed through the curtains of water, and started back toward home.

As Gee leaped around the final bend above the village, he saw Coorah standing on the flat rock where they'd gathered the previous day. She was talking with a new group of platypus warriors. They were skinnier and younger than the other squad of warriors, and they looked nervous, pursing their bills and chewing on their spurs.

Gee couldn't blame them. The ghost bats would arrive within the hour. "Do your tree frogs understand the plan?" he asked Arabanoo.

"Of course they do, you portly mud-puddler."

Gee ribbeted. "You big-toed branch-brain."

"Ground-grubber."

"Leaf-licker!"

They both smiled, then Gee clasped Arabanoo's shoulder. "Take care tonight, Arabanoo."

"You, too. If anything happens to you, your mom will go on a total rampage."

Arabanoo grinned at the thought of Gee's mild-tempered mother rampaging, then leaped onto an overhanging branch, disappearing into the treetops with the rest of his gang.

"Tree toad!" Gee called, then hopped over to Coorah.

"Is the Stargazer still in a trance?" she asked.

"Either that or she really doesn't like me. Is everything ready here?"

Coorah croaked a wry laugh. "That depends on your definition of 'ready.'"

"You know what I mean," Gee said, and glanced

toward the platypus burrows behind the overhanging river roots where the bats had perched during the night.

"Then, yeah." Coorah tossed him a leaf-ball. "Everything's ready."

Gee slitted his nostrils as he felt the weight of the ball. "It's empty?"

"I told you I'm all out of pepperbush goop. At least I finally know how to make it burn on contact, worse than a dozen wasp stings. I'll whip up a new batch when we get back to the Amphibilands." She thought for a second. "I mean, if we survive this."

A platypus nearby moaned. "Don't talk like that."

"We'll be fine," Gee assured him. "Just . . . be ready to move."

The platypus swallowed nervously, then scanned the trees in the sunset. Gee did the same but didn't see any flashes of white among the trunks. The river burbled softly; the wind shook the leaves. The air smelled of fresh water and rich brown earth, like the Amphibilands.

Standing there, waiting for the ghost bats to appear, he suddenly realized that his plan was terrible. It was doomed. Everyone needed to run away right now, to flee to the safety of the burrows! He opened his mouth to say something, and a soft peeping came from the branches above.

"Bats," one of the tree frogs said. "Bats on the way!"

Gee gulped. "Here they come. Everyone get ready."

A moment later, the ghost bats appeared in the dusky woods, flitting like white leaves falling from the trees. Gee drew his club and hung the empty leaf-ball on his belt. Eight of the fastest platypuses in the tribe shifted beside him on the broad flat rock in the shallows. They were unarmed and wide-eyed, and a few were trembling as white wings flapped and flashed through the darkness.

Gee counted ten of the bats, then twenty . . . then he stopped counting. Probably thirty or forty bats, swirling in a pale cloud over the river. An entire legion.

"Oooh, look who's back," one of them hissed. *"Another chance to feed."*

"Things are different tonight," Gee croaked.

"Yesssss," another bat hissed. *"Tonight you won't get away."*

"We'll see about that," Gee said, and flicked his tongue at the bat.

The bat veered away, and a pebble whirred through the air—and missed the bat entirely.

"Too slow!" it hissed at Coorah, who took aim with her slingshot and fired again.

The bat dodged again. *"This time, we know your tricks. Attack!"*

When the swarm of bats streaked toward the rock, Gee leaped at the leader, but two other bats intercepted him. He swung his club and smashed one of them, but the other sank its fangs into his side. He ribbeted in pain, tore free, and crashed to the rock beside Coorah, who was still firing with her slingshot.

"Now?" he asked.

"Not yet," she said, scanning the area. "Are you okay?"

"I've been better," he grumbled, touching his wound. "How about *now*?"

With a quick bulge of her eyes, Coorah checked out the battle, and he did the same. The platypus warriors were squealing and dodging as the bats wheeled and slashed, but they didn't run. And the tree frogs hidden in the branches were quiet and still.

"Now!" Coorah called.

Arabanoo and his tree frogs burst from branches— exactly as they had the previous night. Each of them hurtled toward a bat . . . but this time, the bats were ready. They dodged at the last moment, and the frogs splashed down into the river.

"You can't fool us again!" one bat hissed.

Gee threw his leaf–ball, and it burst open on the bat's head. But without any pepperbush goop inside, it just sort of crumpled there, then fell harmlessly away.

The bat hissed a laugh. *"Attack! Attack! Tonight we feast!"*

The entire swarm of bats swept toward them like a tidal wave.

"Run!" Coorah croaked. "Go!"

The platypuses didn't wait around. They weren't the biggest members of the tribe, but they were the fastest, and before Gee even blinked, they'd slipped into the river. He and Coorah followed an instant later, swimming underwater toward the burrows. Arabanoo and the white–lipped tree frogs floated underwater, waiting for Gee's command, and Gee looked upward, peering through the surface of the water to the air above.

Gee saw the bats streaking toward the roots outside the burrows—just as he'd expected. Because the ghost bats had learned a lesson yesterday. This time, they were going to perch in the roots *before* the frogs and platypuses fled into the riverbank. This time, they were going to keep Gee and the others away from the safety of the burrows. This time, they were going to finish them, once and for all. That was the only strategy that made sense.

Everyone looked to Gee, and he raised a toe pad, telling them to wait in the river. Not a problem for platypuses and frogs. The frogs treaded water, easily staying in place despite the current, while the platypuses wedged themselves beneath rocks: They floated so well that they couldn't stay under for long if they didn't have something holding them down.

Gee peered upward, waiting until the last of the white wisps landed on the roots covering the platypus burrows. Then he broke the surface, and leaped to the riverbank.

Dozens of ghost bats hunched on the tree roots, between him and the safety of the burrows. *"You don't stand a chance against us now,"* one of them whispered. *"Even frogs and platypuses can't stay underwater forever."*

"Well, that part's true," Gee said, shaking himself dry.

"You cannot escape us."

"Don't be so sure," Gee said, as Coorah emerged beside him.

The bat gave a whispery chortle. *"You think escape is possible?"*

"Escape is definitely not possible—" Gee started.

"But you're the ones who are trapped," Coorah finished.

And that's when the ghost bats realized that something was wrong. *"My feet,"* one whispered, suddenly afraid. *"I can't move my feet!"*

"I'm stuck," another said, flapping his wings desperately. *"I'm stuck! I can't fly!"*

"That's because the roots you're standing on are coated in honey," Gee told them politely. "Boiled down and mixed with tree sap."

"No!" the bats screeched. *"Nooo!"*

And Gee yelled: "Attack!"

The frogs and platypuses rose from the river, and ten times as many platypuses burst from the burrows. The ghost bats panicked, flapping their pale wings furiously, yet couldn't lift off. Their clawed feet were too tightly stuck to the roots.

The platypus tribe couldn't beat a flying enemy, but now the bats couldn't fly.

Platypus paws whacked at the ghost bats, and sharp spurs slashed. Gee even saw Pippi slugging a bat with her tail. In a matter of minutes, the battle was over. The ghost bats slumped in sticky, defeated heaps on the roots. The platypus tribe was safe.

21

THE FROGS HOPPED SLOWLY THROUGH the high mountain pass, the icy wind lashing their sensitive skin. Darel stayed near Yabber, whose eyes had been bright with excitement since they'd turned onto the path toward the top of Targangil. He'd been talking nonstop for hours, thrilled at the chance that he might meet the Rainbow Serpent.

And Darel suspected that he was also happy that they were traveling at turtle-speed for once. Without the Komodos, the last leg of the trip had taken five times longer than they'd expected, but it was Ponto who was keeping them to a turtle's pace, because Burnu was leaning on him for support—and grumbling the whole time that Ponto was slowing *him* down.

Darel had offered to help, but Burnu had muttered about muddy-brained wood frogs and said he didn't need any help. So Darel traveled with Yabber, and listened to him babble as they climbed higher and higher into the mountains.

"Some of the old tales claim there are several Rainbow Serpents," Yabber was saying. "Some say it's male, some say it's female—some say it's both! But everyone agrees that the Serpent writhed across the land, creating the hills and valleys and riverbeds—bringing water, and life. But that's not all it brought. Dreamcasting also comes from the Serpent. What is more like a dream than a rainbow, which you see even though it's not there? When we dreamcast, we tap into the power of the Serpent's own dreams, and—"

"Yabber?" Darel interrupted.

"Hmm? Yes? What? Am I talking too much? You know once I start, I have a hard time stopping. My mind races ahead of my mouth, and I talk and talk and—"

"Yabber!"

"I'm doing it again, aren't I?"

Darel gave a croak of laughter. "Why do you think the spider queen tried to slow us down?"

"Ah. Yes. Hmm. Well, that's a fine question. I

suppose she wants to keep us away from the Amphib-ilands."

Darel swallowed. "You think she's already at-tacking?"

"No, I can feel the Veil through my dreamcasting, and she hasn't touched it yet." Yabber lifted his long neck to peer into the distance. "Perhaps she fears the Komodos. Or she's sending more troops to catch us here in the cold. However . . ."

He trailed off, and they moved along in silence until Darel said, " 'However' what?"

"What?" Yabber said, looping his neck back to look at Darel. " 'However what' what?"

Darel almost said, "However what what what?" but he knew that Yabber would keep talking nonsense forever. So he just said, "You said, 'However' . . . "

"Oh! Oh, that's right. However, I have solved *one* riddle. I was wondering, you see, if the rainbow would return . . ."

He gestured upward, and Darel saw it. A huge rainbow arced overhead, bright and clear despite the lack of moisture in the air. The biggest he'd ever seen, gliding endlessly over the clouds, then falling directly onto the mountaintop above.

"Whoa!" he said, his heart suddenly pounding.

"Tickle my toe pads!" Dingo yelled, from up ahead. "Do you see that?"

"You still can't catch a rainbow," Ponto grumbled, though he looked a little uncertain. "It's like trying to drink a mirage."

"Whoa!" Darel repeated, gaping at the rainbow. "That's, that's . . ."

"That's *definitely* a sign," Yabber said, with a little smile.

Although the mountain peak looked close, they climbed for another hour before turning a corner on the rocky path. Then they stopped in amazement. The bright colors of the rainbow were reflected in an untouched field of snow stretching in every direction. The entire world was bathed in a shimmering glow.

For a long moment, nobody moved. Darel gazed at the brilliantly colored field, then flicked his inner eyelids and looked again.

"The end of the rainbow," he said.

Ponto inflated his throat. "That's not . . . possible."

"Yeah," Dingo said, more softly than usual. "That's impossibly awesome."

Because the rainbow fell directly into the center of

the snowy field and ended right there, a hundred feet away. It somehow seemed to be moving or . . . slithering. Darel's heart pounded in his chest. His eyes hurt from bulging, but he just kept staring, dazed with wonder.

Finally, he gulped. "Okay, here goes."

"You're going in?" Dingo asked.

Darel looked at the Kulipari, then at Yabber. "Should I?"

Yabber didn't answer—he was too busy staring with slack-jawed amazement at the rainbow.

"Yes," Quoba told Darel, touching his shoulder. "You should."

"We could all go in."

She shook her head. "I don't think so. This isn't for all of us."

"Why him?" Dingo asked. "Why not me?"

"Because you're a chuckle-bucket," Ponto said. "And he's a . . . Darel."

"He is *such* a Darel," Burnu moaned.

"His father painted the Serpent's message in that cave," Quoba said. "But for whom?"

"You think it's a message for the wood frog?" Burnu asked.

Quoba nodded. "Yeah. That just . . . feels right."

Ponto grunted. "Just feels *cold* to me."

"Take Yabber with you," Quoba told Darel. "And remember one thing."

Darel gulped. "What?"

"This is the greatest honor any frog has been given in many generations."

"But no pressure!" Dingo croaked.

Darel hopped onto the snowy field. The moment he landed, everything changed. The snow around them disappeared. The chill in the air turned to warmth. The snow underfoot transformed into a carpet of grass, and the balmy air carried the perfume of sweet wattle.

The rainbow vanished as well.

For a long moment, Darel simply stood beside Yabber in the middle of what seemed to be a beautiful summer day, feeling warm for the first time since he could remember. His mind was reeling in amazement. Then he saw something glimmering up ahead: a mountain spring, exactly where the rainbow had touched the ground.

"Over there," he said to Yabber, his voice a respectful whisper.

Yabber nodded, and they headed side by side to the spring. There were flowering shrubs along one side of the mountain pool, and insects buzzed from bloom to bloom. Overhead, birds chirped. The grass felt delicious underfoot, and the scent of the water was unlike any Darel had ever smelled before. So fresh and pure that his head swam as they came to the edge of the plain, round pool.

The water was still, and it reflected the blue sky perfectly.

"Can you feel the dreaming?" Yabber asked, softly.

Darel didn't really know what that meant, but he nodded anyway. He sure felt *something*. "What . . . what do we do now?"

"Not even old King Sergu would know that," Yabber said, with a fond smile. "I suppose we ask questions. One moment, and I'll see if my dream-casting can bring the Rainb—"

The mountain pool rippled suddenly, even though there was no wind. Then colors started glinting in the pool, as if reflecting fireworks from above—except when Darel glanced up, he saw nothing but a flat blue sky with a few wispy clouds.

The ripples started lapping against the grass and shrubs, and amid the sloshing, Darel heard a faint watery voice: ". . . water is life . . . in the outback . . ."

"The Rainbow Serpent!" Yabber breathed. Then

he cleared his throat and intoned, "O, Glorious Serpent of Red and Orange and Yellow and Green and, erm, all the other colors, we come with questions of utmost importance—"

"The water runs deep," the splashing murmured. "Deep in the earth. The source of all life . . ."

As the murmuring of the water trailed off, Yabber tried again. "O snakiest of optical phenomena, O mightiest of multicolored archways, will you answer our questions?"

Images rose among the sparkling colors of the pool: a rainstorm over a forest, river rapids whooshing past, a trickle of water running down a muddy gully.

"From above, the rain," the liquid voice gurgled. "From below, deep wells of fresh water."

Shapes shifted in the pool's reflection: In a moment, they looked like brown furry animals swimming in a wide riverbend.

"Is that . . . is that the platypus village?" Yabber asked.

"The rainbow is a sign and a bridge," the splashing continued. "Water is life . . . in the outback."

"Erm, we're quite fond of water ourselves," Yabber

said. "Being turtles and frogs and all of that. But the scorpions and spiders have joined forces. They're trying to take over the Amphibilands, to control all the water—and all the creatures—in the outback."

The ripples in the pool deepened, and Darel caught flashes of his father's reflection: fighting the scorpions, painting the cave, gazing into a mountain pool. Then the water swirled and became an eye—a snake's eye, huge and slitted and glowing with a thousand colors.

The great eye focused on Yabber, and for once the turtle didn't say a word.

Then the eye shifted and stared directly at Darel. His skin started tingling and he forgot how to breathe. The water in the spring started whipping in circles, like a whirlpool. Faster and faster . . .

"You made your journey, Blue Sky King," the watery voice splashed. "Now you seek answers to the deepest questions."

"M-m-me?" Darel inflated his throat, so dazed that he could hardly move. "I . . . I do? I just want to save the Amphibilands."

The whirlpool rose higher and higher, until it was taller than Darel's head, twirling in a spiral like a

tornado. And yet the huge snake eye didn't waver. It kept staring directly at him.

"Water streams through all life," the splashing voice burbled. "Water pools in the cool dark, deep beneath the land—"

A shout sounded, cutting through the stillness.

22

THE SNAKE EYE FINALLY SHIFTED, looking away from Darel.

Startled from his reverie, Darel remembered how to breathe again, remembered how to move. He heard a shout and spun toward the noise . . . and there, through the mist surrounding the flowery meadow, he saw shadowy shapes engaged in battle.

Something was attacking the Kulipari. Something fast and dark and vicious. Before Darel realized what he was doing, he'd pulled his father's dagger from his belt and was crouching low, ready to leap toward the battle.

Except a blinding light stopped him, bright flashes sparkling along his blade. His eyes bulged, and for a moment he thought it was shining from within, with all the colors of the rainbow.

Then he realized that it was reflecting the Serpent, which loomed behind him, stretching up from the little mountain spring and into the sky. For a breathless moment, the Serpent seemed to emerge from the water, higher and higher, endless and magnificent— and then, with one last burst of light, it vanished into the clouds and was gone.

The warm, flowery meadow disappeared. The bees no longer buzzed and the birds no longer chirped. A blanket of snow surrounded Darel and Yabber, the air was as cold as ever . . . and the sun was setting. They must've spent hours staring into the pool without realizing that time was passing. Which meant the Kulipari must've spent hours in the freezing cold. Idly waiting for them, before this attack, which sounded vicious through the mist shrouding the edges of the snowy field.

Darel heard Dingo's shouts and Ponto's ribbets and a few strange, terrible yowling roars. He didn't want to know what animal made that horrible sound, but he knew he was about to find out.

As the last few sparkles faded from his dagger, Darel started to leap forward, but Yabber grabbed his arm. "Wait!"

"What now?" he demanded, anxious to help the Kulipari.

"The spider queen is here. I can feel her night-casting."

"Then let's go kick her abdomen."

"She's more powerful than ever," Yabber said, wrinkling his nose. "I—I—I'm not sure I can stop her."

"Do what you can," Darel told him, though he wasn't sure how changing the weather could possibly help. "The Kulipari will take care of the rest." With that, he bounded away through the snow, toward the fight.

He found the Kulipari five leaps down the mountainside, in an icy ravine. Sloping cliffsides rose on either side of Ponto and Dingo. They stood next to each other, both glowing from their poison. Burnu was slumped against a boulder beside them, weak but still on his feet, one hand raised to catch a boomerang. Quoba stood in front, her colors blazing, her staff a blur in her hands.

At the far end of the gorge, three monsters yowled and spat. They were half as big as the Komodos, with black fur and bulky heads and wide, powerful-looking jaws. Two had white patches on their muscular chests; the other was pure black, and even bigger. Their lips were curled, revealing way too many teeth, and their beady eyes glinted with malice.

And behind them, the spider queen herself. Poison dripped from her fangs. "Where is the turtle?" she

called when she saw Darel. "It's the long-neck freak I want."

"You've got to get past us first," he told her.

Dingo groaned. "Don't encourage her. We're almost out of poison . . ."

"You're strong," Jarrah said, "but you're no match for my devils."

Tasmanian devils! Darel remembered the stories his father had told. The devils were usually kind and peaceful, but the meanest of them sometimes served in other armies as mercenaries. And as the largest meat-eating marsupials in the world, they were fearsome warriors. His father had said that they were a match for even the Kulipari.

Darel hadn't believed a devil could beat a Kulipari then, and he didn't believe it now. So he said, "Yeah? Let's see what you've got."

Queen Jarrah smiled sweetly and plucked one of the strings of her web. A sickening blast of power ricocheted through the ravine, and Darel's confidence wavered. Tasmanian devils were one thing, but Tasmanian devils *plus* a nightcaster sounded like disaster.

He felt his stomach twist at Jarrah's flash of power and heard Ponto grunt beside him. For a moment,

Quoba's bright glow dimmed. Then Dingo spat, "Spiders make me sick," and loosed a volley of arrows at Jarrah.

The spider queen plucked another silken strand, and the arrows fell harmlessly to the floor. She strummed again and again, and an evil force drove the Kulipari backward, sapping their strength, until she murmured to her devils, "Tear them limb from limb."

The devils sprang forward, and at the same time Darel leaped. Midway through his jump, he saw Quoba smash her staff into the biggest devil and heard its roar of anger. Then the second-biggest devil rammed into Ponto. The yellow-and-black glow of Ponto's skin brightened as he strained to keep the devil's teeth from his face.

"Nothing personal, croaker," the devil snarled. "But we've been paid to put you down."

Dingo twirled her bow in her hand and slashed at the devil's ear. It howled, and staggered two steps before the smallest devil slammed into Dingo.

That's when Darel landed on the biggest devil's fat tail. He lifted his dagger, but the devil flicked her tail and he found himself flying through the air, head over toe pad. He hit the wall of the ravine, slid down the rock wall, and slammed into a snowbank.

"Run, little frog," the devil said. "If you want to live."

"I didn't pay you to *advise* them!" Jarrah screamed. "Don't let them run. Kill them! Kill them all, you fur-faced brutes! Earn your money. *Kill them!*"

Darel thought he saw a flicker of doubt in the devil's little eyes, but she yowled a war cry and pounced at him, her crushing jaws opened wide.

He scrambled backward, trying to get his feet beneath him, but the snow was too slippery. The devil lunged forward, snapped her teeth . . . and missed Darel by inches as a boomerang slammed into her snout.

She raised her head to howl in fury, and Darel leaped away. A moment later, he landed beside Burnu. "Thanks!"

Burnu looked weak as he caught his boomerang in a trembling hand. "I've dragged you halfway across the outback, Darel. I'm not going to let some overgrown wombat eat you. But we have to get out of here. Look at the others. Look at Ponto."

His throat inflating anxiously, Darel turned to see Ponto wrestling with a devil. The big frog's yellow stripes were dimming steadily, which meant that his poison was running out. Then the creature shoved forward, teeth bared in triumph, and bulldozed Ponto across the ravine, past Quoba and the biggest devil, who were trading furious blows.

"It's too cold," Burnu murmured. "We can't tap our poison much longer. Quoba's okay for another minute or two, but even Dingo's slowing down."

Fear gripped Darel's heart as he glanced toward Dingo and realized that she'd run out of arrows. He watched as she leaped atop a boulder, shouting, "Hey, you! Tasmaniac! Come to mama, fathead!"

The third devil sprang at her, and she jumped high, clearly planning to somersault in the air and come down hard on the devil's neck . . . But she was too slow. The beast grabbed her foot and flung her to the ground, then whipped her back and forth a few times, smashing her against the rock and ice.

Darel winced. "What should I do?"

"I don't know," Burnu said. "But you're your father's son. So do it *now*."

23

DAREL GRIPPED HIS DAGGER TIGHTLY, glancing between the devil pounding on Ponto and the one tossing Dingo around. "Okay, we need to work as a team. First we take down the one fighting Ponto—"

"I've got this," Quoba said, glowing even more intensely. "I've got *all* of them."

In a moment, she was shining as bright as the sun, and her staff moved too fast for Darel to follow. He'd never seen her tap fully into her poison before; until now, she had always kept to the shadows. He knew she couldn't stay at full power for long, especially in the cold, but it was an awesome sight. She leaped and spun as fast as thought, her staff cracking against the big devil's skull so loudly that the sound echqqoed off the mountains.

The creature staggered backward, and Darel felt himself smile, as hope bloomed in his chest. Even in the freezing cold, the Kulipari were powerful.

But the two other devils were already prowling toward Quoba, growling deep in their throats. She lifted her staff and they paused, raking her with fierce eyes.

"You fight well," the smaller devil growled. "With the heart of a warrior."

"It's a pity that we have to kill you," the other devil said, baring his teeth.

"It's *not* a pity!" the spider queen called, gathering balls of webbing in her hands. "It's a triumph! First the frogs will dangle bloodless in my web, and then the entire outback will feel the lash of my nightcasting! *Get them!*"

As the devils attacked, Jarrah injected venom into the balls of webbing and hurled them across the ravine. They unfurled into thick silken strands that shot toward each of the Kulipari.

Darel lunged in the other direction, planting a webbed foot on the second-biggest devil's forehead. He pushed off, cartwheeling through the air, his dagger slashing downward to stab the third devil from above—but something grabbed his wrist and yanked him backward.

He jerked to a halt, in midair, his left wrist stuck in a spiderweb. As he swung from the web, he saw

Dingo plastered to the floor with webbing, Ponto pinned to the snowy walls of the ravine, and Quoba's color fading as she fought against the sticky nightcast webbing, managing only to further entrap herself. And Burnu was slumped against the boulder, so weak that only the queen's nightcast webbing was keeping him upright.

Darel twisted in the web, raising his arm to slash the sticky silk with his dagger. In a flash, he was surrounded by red eyes, slavering jaws, and black fur. He lowered his arm.

"Where is the turtle?" Jarrah asked him. "He's the one I want."

Darel gulped in fear. "I, um . . ."

"Answer the question! Do you know where the turtle is?"

"S-s-sure," he stammered. "Yes. Yeah."

"Tell me where to find him," she purred, "or I'll have the devils feast. First they'll rip into the Kulipari, then they'll chew your little frog legs for dessert."

Darel inflated his throat in fear. "I'll tell you, I'll tell you!"

"So?" she snapped. "Where is he?"

"Where he always is," Darel said, over the pounding of his heart. "In his shell."

Because Burnu was right. Darel wasn't a real Kulipari, and he'd *never* be a real Kulipari—but he was still his father's son, and he'd never betray a friend.

Jarrah smiled coldly and strummed her web. A blast of prickly magic washed over Darel, and he slumped in the grip of the web, drained and aching.

"Start with the big frog," Jarrah commanded.

The devils slunk across the path to Ponto, lowered their muzzles, then paused. "There is no honor in killing a defeated foe," one said.

"I didn't pay you a hundred glass beads for honor," Jarrah spat.

A faint cough sounded from higher on the mountain path, as soft as a caterpillar's sneeze. Darel twisted his body for a peek . . . and saw Yabber ambling forward, a drowsy look on his face.

"You!" Queen Jarrah sneered, crawling lower on her web.

"Me!" Yabber agreed. "Hullo-ullo-ullo!"

"I've waited a long time for this, you long-neck freak." Jarrah's fangs dripped with poison. "I killed your precious King Sergu, and now I'll kill you. The ancient line of the Serpent's dreamcasters will finally be broken. I'll suck your blood for weeks, then use your shell as my new bathtub."

"No!" Darel strained in his web. She couldn't kill Yabber. He wouldn't let her. "Get away from him!"

"While you've been working on your puny dream-casting," Jarrah snarled, ignoring Darel completely, "I've been plucking the strands of the deepest night-cast webs, gathering power, learning how to weave a web across the entire outback. What have *you* learned? How to teach hatchling turtles to swim?"

"That's silly," Yabber told her, with a drowsy chuckle. "Hatchlings are born knowing how to swim!"

The spider queen raised a hand, and the devils turned from Ponto toward Yabber, powerful shoulders hunched and razor teeth bared.

"You won't be laughing for long." Jarrah spat. "Take him, devils—or I will turn my nightcasting on you!"

The devils narrowed their eyes but prowled toward Yabber.

The long-neck turtle smiled and said, "Hello! I've never met a Tasmanian devil before."

Darel twisted desperately, trying to slash at the sticky web with his dagger. If only he could free himself!

"Oh, and I forgot to mention," Yabber told Jarrah, blinking placidly. "I did learn one thing in the mountains. A spot of weather control."

Jarrah's evil laugh spun into the air. "That won't help you now, turtle."

Darel swiped with his dagger at the webbing, and missed by inches.

"Well, I *do* prefer a nice warm day." Yabber tilted his head. "Do you know one difference between you and us?"

"Yes. *You* will die."

"We like water," Yabber said, and a golden glow shone in his eyes.

The devils pounced at Yabber, and Darel twisted again, stretching his arm and slicing through the web holding him with a single slash. When he fell, his feet splashed in the slush underfoot. He crouched to leap to Yabber's rescue . . . and heard a crashing roar.

As the roar grew louder, Yabber drew his legs into his shell and curved his neck close to his body. "Darel!" he shouted. "Hold on to Burnu!"

The earth began to shake and rumble. Darel didn't know what was happening, but he leaped for Burnu. Halfway there, his eyes bulged when he saw a flood blasting down the path at them, roaring along the ravine. Water. A million gallons, like the waterfall in the Amphibilands thundering down, five times higher than Darel was tall.

He grabbed Burnu, and the raging river hit. First it lifted Yabber high; then it sucked him low. The white water flattened all three devils, then swept over Dingo and Ponto and Quoba, ripping them free from the webs. The torrent slammed closer, and Darel's entire body clenched in fear. He hugged Burnu close, sticking tight with his toe pads, waiting for the icy water to hammer them.

Then the wave hit, tumbled him—and the water was warm!

Warm and almost . . . gentle. Heated by Yabber's weather-control dreamcasting.

From the outside, the water looked like a raging flood, but once he was submerged, once he was *part* of the torrent, it felt more like a ride than a death trap. Holding onto Burnu, he pushed off the ravine wall and found a fast, warm current that carried him down the mountain like he was surfing underwater.

Quoba drifted past, upside down and doing a feeble frog-stroke, and a moment later Ponto sort of lumbered underneath Darel, bubbles streaming behind him as he weakly hop-swam through the cascading water. A flicker of motion caught Darel's eye, and he saw Dingo flailing around underwater, plucking her used arrows from the current.

The warmth of the water had woken them up a little or at least given them enough energy to swim instead of drown. Even Burnu's snakebite didn't seem so inflamed.

Then Darel saw the Tasmanian devils. Apparently, the water didn't feel so warm and gentle to them. Devils were usually strong swimmers, but this mountain flood was smashing them around like pebbles in a hollow gourd. They slammed against the ravine wall, then plunged into the rocky riverbed, hurtled into the

air, bounced off crags and outcroppings, and splashed back into the churning water.

After hefting Burnu to the surface for a breath, Darel caught a glimpse of shimmering silken threads. At the other end of the webbing, Jarrah thrashed her arms desperately. Spiders didn't swim at the best of times—and this definitely wasn't the best of times. She was flailing all eight limbs, and her mouth was wide open in a silent scream. She looked like a panicked cockroach.

Darel lost sight of her as Yabber swam past, in his slow, turtle-ish way. For a moment, Darel stared: Yabber's eyes were now a pure gold, just like old King Sergu's.

While he was gaping, Yabber mouthed a few words, which Darel somehow understood: "I melted the snow on the mountaintop! Weather control *rocks*!"

24

EE GRABBED A ROOT AND SWUNG over the river. "Look out below!" he cried.

He let go of the root, did a somersault in midair, and splashed down beside Coorah.

"Hey!" She flicked her tongue and thwacked the side of his head. "Some of us are floating here!"

"Some of us are *swimming*," Pippi called, zooming past. "Slowpokes!"

For a fuzzy critter with a chubby tail, Pippi moved surprisingly fast in the water. Gee laughed and swam after her. In the background he could hear the music of the celebration in the village. The platypus tribe really knew how to throw a party. There was singing and feasting, dancing and games and stories.

Plus, the entire village was treating the frogs like heroes. Cheering for them and carrying them around and, well, feeding them. Gee tried to be humble, but he had to admit he enjoyed basking in the admiration. And eating. He *always* enjoyed eating.

As Pippi started racing with her sister, he lazily drifted back to Coorah. "This is the life, huh?"

"You said it." She smiled, then turned thoughtful. "I never thought I'd see the world outside of the Amphibilands. I sure never imagined it'd be like *this*."

"Yeah, I figured it was all deserts and scorpions."

"You know what's weird?"

Gee looked across the river at Arabanoo and his gang, who were in the branches singing along with a platypus song. "Tree frogs?" he said.

"No!" Coorah shoved him. "What's weird is that the Veil doesn't just keep *danger* out—it keeps *us* in. I'd never really thought of that before."

Gee inflated his throat slowly. "Me, neither. Of course, it also keeps us alive."

"That's true." She smiled as Pippi and her sister swam past. "I'm glad we came. I'm glad we helped, and I'm glad we got to see all of this."

"Yeah," Gee said. "Darel would love this. I wonder where he is."

They didn't speak for a while, watching the festivities. Platypups played games in the shallows while

older platypuses slid noisily down a mudslide. Fresh-caught crawdads were passed around as the adult platypuses chatted about fishing and burrows and the defeat of the ghost bats.

Pippi burst from the water beside Gee with a sudden splash. "Hey, guess what!"

He clutched his chest. "Don't scare me like that."

"She's awake!"

"Who is?"

"The Stargazer, silly!"

"Oh." He gazed upstream. "Is she coming to the party?"

"She's already at the fire circle. Come on, I'll introduce you. Nobody tells better stories than she does." As they climbed the riverbank to the clearing, Pippi launched into some nutty tale about a crocodile who cheated the sun, then she paused, seeing all the older platypuses clustered around the fire. "Excuse me!" she said, wriggling through the crowd. "Frogs crossing! Pardon my bill . . ."

When they reached the front, Gee saw the gray-furred Stargazer standing atop a stump. She was so old and stooped that she barely reached the top of the taller platypuses' heads, and she squinted as though she couldn't see very well. But when she spoke in her soft voice, everyone fell completely silent to hear.

"I've been listening to rainbows," she started.

Gee bulged his eyes at Coorah. *Listening* to rainbows? That was strange, even for a platypus.

"And watching the sounds of the river," the Stargazer continued. "The Rainbow Serpent is restless, shining and slithering, tasting the future with a flick of its tongue. At first, I didn't understand. What was causing this restlessness?"

She grew quiet, and her gentle gaze swept the crowd. She seemed to linger for a moment on Coorah's face, and then on Gee's, and he thought he saw a reflection of a thousand rainbows in her eyes.

Then she continued, "There is a terrible darkness coming to the tribe, the likes of which we've never seen before. We are in deadly danger, and very soon now—"

"It already came!" Pippi blurted. "The ghost bats came and they hunted us, and the frogs helped fight them and we—"

"Hush, Pippi," the Stargazer said. "I am speaking of something worse than ghost bats."

"Was Jarrah behind them?" Gee asked. "Is *she* coming?"

"She brought the scorpion lord back from the dead," the Stargazer said. "Stronger. Crueler. Deadlier than ever. Deadlier than *her*. And when Marmoo comes, death will come with him."

"What . . . what should we do?" an older platypus asked.

"Flee."

"But when? Now? The frogs beat Marmoo last time, Stargazer . . . Stargazer?"

The Stargazer was peering into the sky. The crowd fell quiet, and everyone waited for her answer. The platypuses shifted and curled their bills, but still she didn't answer. She simply gazed at the clouds.

Gee slitted his nostrils. The Stargazer seemed nice and all, but he wished she didn't fall into a daze every time someone asked her a question. How would the platypuses save themselves? And what about the Amphibilands?

"We can fight it!" one of the younger platypuses said.

"You heard what the Stargazer said," another told him. "We can't fight something worse than ghost bats . . . worse than the spider queen."

"We can if the frogs help!"

The platypuses turned toward Gee and Coorah.

With a nervous flick of his inner eyelids, Gee glanced at Coorah and muttered, "What do we say?"

"I don't know," she whispered.

Gee cleared his throat. "Can . . . can the Stargazer tell us anything more?" he asked, loudly. "What does 'very soon' mean? *How* soon?"

"She probably doesn't know," Pippi replied. "She sees only bits and pieces in her trances. She says it's like trying to track a single drop of rain in a monsoon."

"*Can* you help us?" one of the platypuses asked, looking from Gee to Coorah.

"I'm not sure," Coorah said, frowning slightly. "We barely beat the bats, and Darel tricked Marmoo—I'm afraid to think how powerful he is *now*."

"I'm not afraid to fight!" a voice called.

"Me, neither!" another called. "This is our home!"

"I won't leave my burrow without a fight!" a third voice shouted.

"The frogs will save us again!"

"*Say* something." Coorah nudged Gee. "This isn't safe."

He swallowed. "Why me?"

"Because you're Darel's sidekick?"

"Oh, fine." He raised his voice and said, "Um!"

Then he trailed off. He didn't know what else to say.

"I think you can do better than '*Um*,'" Coorah told him, with a quick glare.

"Sheesh." Gee took a deep breath and tried to think what Chief Olba would say. And just like that, the answer popped into his mind. "Listen! Everyone listen to me! We'll send our fastest frog to the Amphibilands, to ask Chief Olba what to do!"

"Ooooh," Pippi said. "I met her. She's really smart."

"Hey, that's actually a good idea," Coorah said, sounding a little surprised.

Gee stuck his tongue out at her as the platypuses started to chat among themselves. After a few minutes, they nodded and murmured their agreement. "Yes, that sounds best," one said.

"I guess I'll start hopping, then," Gee said. "It'll take me all night to get home."

Coorah laughed. "You? I thought you said our *fastest* frog?"

"I *am* our fastest frog."

"Fastest at what, eating?" She nudged him again. "You *know* I'm faster than you."

"Well, maybe a little."

"And so is Arabanoo. And . . . well, everyone else."

"Not everyone," Gee objected.

"I'll go," Coorah said. "I want to start on a new batch of pepperbush goop anyway."

"Fine!" Gee croaked, trying to lighten the mood with a joke. "I'll guard the buffet table until you get back."

25

AREL FLICKED HIS INNER EYELIDS to clear his vision. He held tight to Burnu as an eddy inside the surging river sloshed them around hairpin turns and whizzed them along rocky gullies. Even though he used to surf the waterfall back home for fun, he felt a little dizzy.

Finally, they tumbled down a long waterfall and into a deep rock-lined pool.

For a moment, Darel didn't know which way was up. They'd covered three days' journey in one long, crazed blast that ended with a huge splash into a pond at the foot of the mountain range. He followed the bubbles to the surface, still holding Burnu, dazed and dizzy and trying to catch his breath.

A cliff loomed behind him, and the outback stretched ahead—miles of scrub and bush between him and the Amphibilands. He floated there, battered and exhausted and relieved, drinking the fresh, pure mountain water through his skin.

Then Burnu muttered something, and Darel remembered the snakebite.

"Are you okay?" he asked, paddling for the edge of the pond. "I'll get some herbs and—"

"I *said*," Burnu mumbled, "stop dragging me around like a sack of pebbles."

"Sheesh," Darel said. "I'm only trying to help."

"Mud-belly," Burnu snorted.

"Hey, I saved your butt from that flash flood."

"Still not a real Kulipari," Burnu said, and fainted.

"Set him down here," Yabber called as he climbed onto dry land nearby. "I'll check his bite."

Darel blinked at the sight of Yabber's now-golden eyes, then dragged Burnu from the pool, and sat heavily beside him, panting. A second later, Ponto and Quoba crawled feebly from the water and collapsed beside Yabber.

"Owww," Ponto moaned. "I'm one big bruise."

"And I'm a series of little bruises," Quoba groaned. "Next time we do that, remind me not to run out of poison."

"We're not doing that again," Ponto said. "Not ever. You'd have to be crazier than a kookaburra to do *that* again."

"Woo-*hoooooo*!" Dingo yelped, careening down

the waterfall in a swell of water. "Look at me! I'm a frogalanche! I'm a—"

She smacked into the pool, and the sound echoed like a tree limb cracking.

Darel winced. "Well, that must've hurt."

A second later Dingo emerged from the pool, sputtering and unsteady. "—a Kuli-*pour*-i!" She finished her pun, then collapsed onto the shore.

"At least we're all alive," Darel told Yabber.

"Barely," Yabber told Darel, with a frown. "Look at Burnu. And the rest don't have enough poison left to fight off an angry possum."

"Can I help? I'll get herbs or—"

Quoba pointed over Darel's shoulder. "The devils!"

Darel spun and saw them staggering unsteadily from the water, claws scrabbling in the dirt as they heaved themselves onto dry land, ears drooping and black fur soaked. One of them shook weakly, and Darel flicked his inner eyelids against the spray of water. He watched them warily, ready to reach for his dagger at a moment's notice.

The biggest one stared at him across the water, her mean eyes narrowing. "For a bunch of pond-piddlers, you sure can fight."

"Yeah," one of the smaller devils said. "And that Jarrah is battier than a bandicoot."

"She paid us well, though . . ."

The big one shrugged. "She's got more crazy than she's got legs. She wants to trap the entire outback in her web?"

"She threatened you, too," Darel said. "If you keep working for her, she'll suck you dry."

The big devil shook water from her fur. "The hopper's got a point. It's not worth the money. I'm done with spiders. Let's haul whisker out of here."

The devils turned and lumbered away across the foothills.

Darel watched until they disappeared, and then he slumped in relief and gazed at the water still cascading down the mountainside. The memory of the Rainbow Serpent's pool rose in his mind, but despite meeting the Serpent and escaping Jarrah, he felt tendrils of worry coiling in his stomach. They hadn't stopped the threat to the outback. And Marmoo was still out there somewhere. Plotting and planning . . . growing more powerful.

Darel sighed as he watched the waterfall. He needed to—

His thoughts screeched to a halt when a silken

strand of nightcast webbing shot from the top of the waterfall and scraped across the sky.

"Over there!" he said, pointing. "Look!"

The thread grew longer and longer, rising higher and higher in an updraft until it yanked Queen Jarrah from the torrent, halfway down the waterfall. She was coughing and trembling, and two of her legs were bent the wrong way.

"I'll kill you all!" she shrieked as she ballooned away. "Wrap you in my web, every frog and turtle, every platypus and dreamcaster! I know you spoke to that filthy Serpent!

"I'll burn the platypus village to the ground. We'll march on them today, and you'll *never* discover what the Serpent wants . . ."

She continued ranting as she floated out of earshot.

"That's the last straw," Dingo muttered. "I am so not inviting her to my birthday party."

"We've got to get moving," Darel declared. "We might already be too late."

"Get moving *where*?" Ponto blinked at him. "We can barely hop, Darel."

"You heard Jarrah. She and Marmoo are attacking the platypus village next—not the Amphibilands. She needs to stop the platypus Stargazer, so nobody can understand the Rainbow Serpent."

"Yes," Yabber said, nodding slowly. "She wants to neutralize our most powerful ally."

"She's going to burn the village down." Darel frowned. "She's going to kill them all."

"You're right," Yabber said, his voice troubled and his golden eyes shining. "We must move quickly. I see . . . I see . . ."

"You see what?" Ponto grumbled. "What do you see?"

"I see death," Yabber told him. "The death of someone we love. And a peaceful land destroyed."

26

"HANKS SO MUCH, GEE," PIPPI'S MOM said with a smile. "You're a huge help."

Gee looked up from the root he was repairing. It had broken during the battle with the bats. "My parents are builders. I grew up working with wood."

"What do they build?"

"Homes, mostly. Bungalows and leaf cottages and tree houses."

"How lovely. Our tribe does construction as well. Although we focus on excavation."

"What's that?"

"Digging. In the old days, they say the Rainbow Serpent asked us to dig long tunnels crisscrossing the land, with cisterns and siphons, to carry water from the Amphibilands to the rest of the outback."

Gee wasn't sure what a cistern was, but he was embarrassed to ask after not knowing "excavation." "Wow. The Serpent actually talked to you?"

"That's what the stories say, and—" She peered up the riverbank. "Hmm. My bill is tingling, I think someone's coming."

Gee set his tools aside and grabbed his club. He leaped to the clearing beneath the spreading tree branches, then ribbeted in surprised pleasure. "Chief Olba! You're here!"

The old frog hopped forward, her black skin gleaming and her red-crowned forehead bright. She gave him a hug. "Of course. As soon as Coorah told me what the Stargazer said."

"Told *us*," Old Jir said, leaning on his cane nearby. "Good job with the ghost bats, by the way."

"Thanks."

"Not such a good job keeping watch, though," Old Jir continued, his pale eyes bulging. "There's a terrible danger looming, and we hopped right into the village without anyone raising the alarm."

"Well, we *are* frogs," Chief Olba told him, gesturing to the ten bullfrog warriors standing with Coorah. "The platypuses know we're friends."

"What are you going to tell them?" Gee asked her.

"The Stargazer says the danger is coming soon—and they don't have the Veil to protect them."

"I'll tell them to grab what they need and come to

the Amphibilands," the chief said. "They can stay as long as they want. There's plenty of room, and plenty of water."

But a short while later, after she had made her announcement, one of the platypuses called out, "We can't leave the village! We were born here. Our parents were born here. Our grandparents were born here. Our great-grandparents were—"

"It's the only way to keep your platypups safe," Chief Olba interrupted. "Once they're inside the Veil, nothing can hurt them."

At least not until the scorpions burst through the tear in the Veil, Gee thought, but he kept it to himself.

"That's true," the platypus said with a thoughtful nod.

"We've got to keep the pups safe," another said. "Nothing's more important than that."

"So you must leave immediately." Olba gestured to the bullfrogs and said, "My frogs will help you gather what you need."

As she spoke, Gee hopped away, his throat puffed in thought. Old Jir was right: With danger coming, they definitely needed sentries.

— ✳ —

Commander Pigo skittered across the parched earth, his main eyes peering into the distance. The dry desert wind felt soothing on his carapace after having been so long in the spider queen's castle, and the scent of sandalwood and bluebush helped him forget the stink of rotting flies.

He caught a glimmer of motion from the direction of the distant Snowy Mountains and raised a pincer, bringing the scorpion squad to a halt behind him.

"There!" He tilted his head and peered at the sky. "What is that?"

"Not a hawk, sir," one of the soldiers said.

"It's a spider," Pigo said, eying the floating speck. "What do they call it? Ballooning?"

"Haven't all the spiders returned from the Snowy Mountains?" the soldier asked, shading his main eyes with his pincer.

"They have," Pigo said. "So stay ready. This might be a Kulipari trap."

Pigo led his squad closer to the ballooning spider, and he saw that it was the *queen* lofting high above. As he watched, Jarrah started unspooling more webbing from her spinnerets, and at last she swirled to the ground fifty feet from where he stood.

When Pigo reached her, she looked half-dead. Her face was bruised, two legs were broken, and blood seeped through her silken gown.

"Lift her onto your backs!" he ordered his soldiers. "Bring her along, double time!"

They headed for the encampment, where Lord Marmoo and the queen's servants were awaiting her return. The spider guards caught sight of their injured queen and called for her ladies-in-waiting, who bustled forward and laid healing strands of silk across her face.

Commander Pigo sidled beside Lord Marmoo and muttered, "She is badly hurt, m'lord."

"What a pity." Marmoo's mouthparts moved into a smile. "Tell the soldiers to get into position. You stay with me."

Marmoo skittered toward Jarrah, each of his steps now twice as long as Pigo's. Perhaps his carapace was soft, but he moved with a killing grace that made even Pigo tremble. Still, he stayed close as Marmoo loomed over the ladies-in-waiting who were treating the queen.

Jarrah lay on a silken stretcher, surrounded by shimmering threads. "Marmoo," she gasped, when she saw him. "That turtle freak tricked me . . . the devils betrayed me."

"And the Kulipari?"

Jarrah closed her eyes. "Injured and weakened . . ."

"But alive?"

"Yes."

"Are they still in the mountains?"

"No," Jarrah said, opening her eyes into slits. "They're . . . they're headed for the platypus tribe."

"They told you where they're going?" Marmoo asked, and Pigo heard the suspicion in his voice.

She smiled weakly. "No, I told them where *we're* going. They'll be desperate to protect the platy- puses—the beloved children of the Rainbow Serpent. We'll meet them there, and finish this once and for- ever."

"An excellent plan," Marmoo said. "As long as you harden my carapace first."

"Not yet," she said, with a shiver. "Not while I'm so weak."

Marmoo's tail flashed, and his razor-tipped stinger touched Jarrah's throat. "Harden my shell, Jarrah, or I will kill you where you lie."

"Kill me and you'll never reach your full power."

"Liar!" The stinger pressed into her flesh. "Pigo told me that you can *speed* the transformation, but that it will happen anyway. Sadly for you, I'm not feeling patient—or merciful. Do it now!"

"I can't," she said. "I need my castle. I need—"

"I know what you need. Only your webbing and venom. You kept me weak, Jarrah, and I despise weakness. You have five seconds."

She looked into his merciless eyes, then nodded. "I'll do as you say, but beware, Marmoo. You will pay for this."

"Once you harden my carapace," he said, his tone almost as silken as hers, "I'll be in your debt. First we'll kill the Kulipari and that dreamcaster—then we'll take the Amphibilands."

She glared at him, her face sharp and angry. "I will take more than the wetlands."

"Fine," Marmoo said, clearly trying to sound reasonable. "We'll take the entire outback. You will spread your nightcast web from mountain to desert to coast. Or you'll die right here."

After a venomous pause, Jarrah started pulling silk from her spinnerets. "Wrap this around yourself."

"Commander," Marmoo barked, "take my place."

Pigo stepped forward and put his stinger against the queen's neck while Marmoo spun, wrapping himself in a loose weave of spider silk. Pigo watched carefully, remembering what the ladies-in-waiting had told him.

"Now the venom," Pigo said, when he thought there was enough webbing.

Jarrah narrowed her eyes, but did as he instructed. As she dripped venom onto the silken thread, a tendril of smoke rose from where the poison splashed down. The smoke seemed to writhe along the webbing, coiling around Lord Marmoo's legs and his stinger, his pincers and his shoulders, then his back and his underbelly.

Through the webbing, Pigo watched the pale gray of Marmoo's carapace turning dark brown. Then black.

The desert wind died down. There was silence on the plateau.

Then Lord Marmoo stretched to his full height, spreading his pincers and straightening his tail. He ripped the silken webbing from his body. His carapace gleamed, blacker than black, so dark that it swallowed the daylight. His tail curved wickedly, each armored segment swaying slightly. His plated legs were thick with muscle.

Pigo stepped back in awe, then bent his front legs and bowed deeply. The other scorpions bowed as well, and Pigo caught a ripple of motion in his side eyes as the spider warriors did likewise.

Only Queen Jarrah seemed unimpressed. "Very well," she said. "Now you are fully reborn, Marmoo. You must travel to the platypus village and wipe them out. Them, the Kulipari, and the dreamcaster. Nobody else can stop me. You must—"

Marmoo's stinger blurred forward and stabbed into Jarrah's side. His venom pumped and she went completely limp in an instant. Dead.

He grabbed the body in one pincer and held it high for everyone to see. "I am Marmoo," he called. "Lord of the scorpions *and* the spiders. Lord of the desert, lord of the swamp, lord of the outback. Let any who oppose me speak now."

The silence seemed to deepen, and Pigo imagined he could taste fear in the air. If anyone even whispered, they would die.

And he tasted his own fear as well. He knew that Lord Marmoo would tear down the Veil and lead the scorpions to a land of bottomless water holes and bountiful valleys. Nothing mattered more than that. But part of him looked upon this new Lord Marmoo and trembled: Marmoo was no longer a Scorpion Lord; he'd turned himself into a Scorpion God.

"And now, Pigo," Marmoo said, his voice soft again, "we rip the platypus village to shreds and wait for the Kulipari to arrive."

"And then you'll kill them all, m'lord?"

"With ease," Marmoo said. "And the Amphibilands will be completely undefended."

27

EE SHOT HIS TONGUE AT A PASSING grasshopper, then headed for a weedy hill, munching absentmindedly. When he reached the top, he climbed along a jagged ridge and peered at the outback, his eyes bulging. Nothing in sight but the endless desert and the mountains, barely visible far in the distance.

He paced for a while, inflating his throat periodically, then he sat against the trunk of a cypress tree and chewed on a smoked beetle that Pippi's father had given him. Pretty tasty, he had to admit. The platypuses liked strong flavors as much as they liked floating in the river. Hmm. Those were two of Gee's favorite things, too. Maybe he was actually a platypus. A non-goofy one, of course, without a silly bill or a coating of fur.

He leaned back, thinking about the village. He wondered if they were done packing. He wondered if they had any food left over from the party. Then he yawned. Sentry duty was boring, but that didn't matter. He narrowed his eyes. He was a warrior, he'd stay sharp and alert . . .

A faint rattling sound startled him, and he blinked himself awake.

Wait. *Awake*? He'd been watching, not sleeping.

That's when he realized that he was curled on his side beneath the cypress, and had covered himself in a thin blanket of leaves. *Oops. Must've dozed off,* he thought. He shook briskly, then narrowed his eyes, gazing toward the outback.

And the rattling sound came again. From where? The gorge on the other side of the ridge. Something was creeping forward, sneaky and furtive.

Gee drew his club as he slipped behind the cypress trunk. He sucked in his gut, took a few deep breaths, then stuck one eye around the trunk. What was there? A spider? A snake? A scorpion?

He saw nothing. Silence fell. Should he run for it? No. If he ran, whatever it was would chase him. And anyway, he needed to know if it was a scorpion scout or something else. He swallowed nervously. Or something *worse*.

He peeped around the tree again—and the sneaky

shape burst over the ridge, launching through the air toward him.

Too late to run! He *had* to stand and fight.

With a terrified war bellow, Gee leaped at the shape, swinging his club with all his might. They met in the air, two warriors crashing together with a thunderclap, in an amazing display of military might.

Well, or at least they would have, if, at the very last moment, the sneaking thing hadn't yelled, "Gee! It's you!"

It caught Gee in a massive hug, and they slammed to the ground together.

Gee blinked his inner eyelid in disbelief. "Darel?"

"It's you! It's you!" Darel hopped a few times. "Hey, everyone! It's Gurnugan!"

"Darel!" Gee cried, and this time *he* hugged Darel—so hard that his eyes bulged. "What happened? What are you doing out there? Did you find Yabber?"

"Yeah, we found him, but—"

"Thank frog!" Gee said, and even though he knew he was babbling, he couldn't stop himself. "We're in trouble. Big trouble. Where are the Kulipari? They'll fix this! Are they rested? Are they ready? Are they raring to rip into battle?"

"Not exactly," Darel said, pulling Gee toward the ridge. "They're down there."

Gee looked over the ridge and saw them in the gorge below.

Yabber was trudging along, his long neck drooping. He looked like a pack animal, with Burnu sprawled across his shell. Burnu's chest was wrapped in bandages, and his head lolled to one side. Ponto hopped wearily along, his shoulders slumped and a bandage on his arm. Even Dingo, who usually had more energy than a tadpole nursery, looked limp and exhausted.

Only Quoba seemed healthy, hopping along in front. Except Gee realized that he had spotted her immediately. Usually she scouted so stealthily that you didn't notice her until she was three inches away.

"Yikes!" Gee said. "What happened to them?"

"Tasmanian devils. And the spider queen."

Gee winced. "Ouch."

"Yeah. But what do you mean, 'big trouble'? I—" Darel stopped suddenly and grinned. "I can't believe it's you!"

"Because I'm so much tougher than when you saw me last?"

"Gee, I saw you last week."

"A lot's happened since then." Gee crooked his arm. "Want to feel my muscles?"

"No, I don't want to feel your—"

"You've got to! You're my sidekick."

"I'm your *what*?"

"My sidekick."

Darel snorted. "Okay, now I believe it's you."

"Here." Gee dug in his pouch and tossed a honeyed worm into the air. "This'll prove it."

Darel flicked his tongue to catch the worm, and chewed appreciatively. "Mmm. Sweet and sticky."

"That's how the platypuses like 'em," Gee said.

"The platypuses?" Darel blinked. "You met a platypus?"

"That's what I'm saying, Darel. They're under attack. Something is coming for the platypus tribe."

"Yeah, Jarrah and Marmoo."

Gee gaped at him. "You already know?"

"That's where we're heading. We heard about it after we left the mountains. But the Kulipari are . . . not strong right now."

"Well, maybe they won't have to fight for a while." Gee inflated his throat. "The chief's at the village, helping the platypuses move to the Amphibilands."

"Chief Olba?" Darel asked.

"Yeah. She says that whatever threat's coming—"

"Oh, *no*!" Darel gasped, grabbing Gee's arm. "The threat's not just coming, Gee. It's *ahead* of us."

28

WITH HIS PULSE RACING, DAREL shaded his eyes and peered across the outback. A column of spiders and scorpions marched steadily through the brush toward the woods that surrounded the river. Toward the platypus village. Closer than Darel and the frogs. And the worst part was the scorpion in front: a fearsome glossy black scorp who shone with power.

"Is th-th-that *Marmoo*?" Gee croaked, dryly. "I heard the rumors that he was still alive, but I don't remember him being so . . . huge."

"He wasn't." Darel made his eyes bulge so he could look closer. "He's twice as big now. See that stinger?"

"And his carapace! He's better armored than a Komodo."

Darel nodded. "He looks worse than Jarrah. Way worse."

"So much for the Kulipari not having to fight for a while," Gee said.

"I'm not sure if they *can* fight." Darel hopped to the ridge, then called to the Kulipari in the gorge. "Everyone get up here! You need to see this."

They looked at him for a second, then Ponto eased the unconscious Burnu to the ground while Dingo flopped down on a nearby rock and started rubbing her toe pads. The two of them were too beat to even make it up the hill.

Only Yabber and Quoba climbed the ridge to join Darel and Gee, who stood in silence, watching Marmoo lead his soldiers into the fringes of the woods, on the path to the platypus village.

"Where's Jarrah?" Gee asked.

"She's dead," Yabber said. He stretched out his neck and peered toward the woods. "I felt her fade away. She did a casting moments before she died, and now I see why—she was pouring her dark magic into Marmoo."

"We've got to get to the village," Darel said. "And fast."

"Marmoo's ten minutes closer than we are," Gee said, flicking his inner eyelids. "Maybe Dingo can beat him."

"Dingo couldn't beat a slug right now," Darel said. "The fight with the devils sapped her power."

"Well, we need the Kulipari."

"I'm afraid," Yabber said, slowly, "that the Kulipari are tapped out."

"Completely?" Gee asked.

Yabber nodded. "If Ponto and Dingo use their poison, they will most certainly lose their power—forever. And Quoba's not doing much better."

Darel put his hand on Gee's arm. "It's down to you and me, Gee. We're not Kulipari, but we'll get the job done."

"Just like old times!" Gee said, and his voice only trembled a little.

"I'm coming," Quoba said, hopping beside them. "Maybe I can't use my poison, but I'm still faster than a couple of wood frogs."

"We'll see about that!" Darel said, trying to smile. Then he looked to Yabber. "Any advice before we go?"

Yabber closed his golden eyes. "Don't try to fight Marmoo. He's too strong. Just lead the platypuses to safety. I sense death on the path ahead, and . . . a peaceful land left empty."

"The platypus village?" Gee asked, his nostrils slitted in worry. "Or the Amphibilands?"

"Maybe both," Yabber replied, shaking his head slowly. "I don't know—the vision is hazy. Talk to the Stargazer, Darel. Find out what she knows. And be careful, all of you."

"We will," Darel promised. Then he patted Yabber on the shell for good luck, and leaped away.

29

WHEN LORD MARMOO PAUSED, Pigo raised his pincer, and the troops halted behind him. The scent of fresh water drifted toward them, and Pigo watched Marmoo's mouthparts curl into a smile. The platypus village was nothing compared to the Amphibilands—just one short stretch of river and some nasty, soggy forest—but it made a tasty appetizer on the way to the main course.

"Soon the river will run red with the blood of the platypus tribe," Marmoo said.

"Yes, m'lord," Pigo said.

"And when the Kulipari come to save them, I'll wipe those croakers from the face of the earth." He snapped a pincer. "Then we attack through the rip in the Veil, with nobody to stop us! We seize the frogs' water and feast on their young."

He gestured for half his army to flank him on

the right and the other half to fan out on his left. Pigo followed a half step behind his lordship, skittering toward the scent of water until the sound of the river burbled through the trees.

Followed by the sound of platypus voices.

Creeping closer, Pigo parted a thicket of branches and saw a wide riverbend. To his surprise, there weren't any platypuses swimming in the water: Instead, a line of them stretched from the riverbank into the woods. And they were carrying heavy packs, even the youngest platypups.

"They're running away!" Marmoo growled to Pigo.

"Someone must've warned them."

"*Someone* betrayed me," Marmoo snarled. His side eyes glared at Pigo, and his stinger quivered with the eagerness to strike.

Pigo willed his mid-legs to stop trembling. "Th-th-the Rainbow Serpent, my lord?"

Marmoo frowned. "What?"

"Was it the Rainbow Serpent, my lord? Could it have warned the platypuses?"

"Hmm." Marmoo relaxed his stinger. "Yes, that makes sense. Not that it matters. The multicolored meddler is too late. None of these platypuses will survive."

"Yes, my lord," Pigo said. "And once you kill the Kulipari, the froglands will be defenseless against you."

"Speaking of frogs." Marmoo's mouthparts curved as a handful of armed bullfrogs appeared among the platypuses. "I spy a few tasty ones there . . ."

He shoved through the branches, then stopped and gave a low, slithery laugh that reminded Pigo of Queen Jarrah. Because the platypuses were on the *other* side of the river. Spiders and scorpions couldn't swim across.

"Pigo," Marmoo murmured. "Tell the troops to build a bridge. By the time you cross, there will be enough meat for an army."

"And you, my lord? Can you swim now?"

Marmoo's eyes flashed with bloodlust. "I don't need to swim."

He burst from the cover of the trees and skittered toward the river. Pigo saw horror on the faces of the platypuses as Marmoo sped to the edge of the riverbank, crouched, and with all his new strength, leaped across the river. He soared through the air, his pincers wide and his tail coiled to strike.

The young platypuses shrieked, and a few of the

older ones swiveled toward the invader, their bills pinched with fear.

Marmoo splashed into the shallows, and three big platypuses jumped him, swinging the poison spurs on their hind legs.

With a low laugh, Marmoo effortlessly dodged his attackers. He lashed out with stinger and pincers, and in a moment the creatures had scattered.

"The faster you run," he taunted, his voice carrying easily across the river, "the more fun I will have hunting you!"

Pigo called a few orders to his soldiers, instructing them to drag a log across the narrowest part of the river. When he looked back, he saw a motherly-looking platypus stepping toward Lord Marmoo.

"W-w-why?" the platypus asked, shivering slightly. "Why are you doing this?"

"You're just bait," Marmoo said, sliding closer. "To draw out the Kulipari. And any friend of the Rainbow Serpent is an enemy of mine."

"Please, we don't mean you any harm."

Marmoo touched his stinger to the platypus's face. "You couldn't harm me if you tried."

"Get away from my mom!" a platypup cried, and rushed at Marmoo from behind.

"No!" one of the male platypuses shouted. "Pippi, no!"

Pigo winced as Marmoo kicked with a rear leg and sent the platypup flying backward. The mother platypus screamed, and his lordship grinned. "Is that your pup? I'll save her for last."

He moved to strike the motherly platypus with his stinger when Pigo caught sight of three spears ripping through the air toward him.

"My lord!" he called, in warning.

But there was no need. With a slash of his pincer, Lord Marmoo snapped one of the spears in half in midair. The other two struck his side . . . and splintered into a thousand pieces.

Spears couldn't pierce Marmoo, not anymore, and Pigo felt a strange sense of dread. He knew he should celebrate his master's invincibility, but instead an uneasy fear roiled in his gut. He swallowed his unease, snapped a few commands at the bridge-building soldiers, then swiveled back to the battle.

The bullfrogs who'd thrown the spears had drawn swords and were circling Lord Marmoo. They looked tiny compared to him—and the tree frogs in the branches above looked even smaller.

Marmoo raised his pincers as if he was surrendering. "Oh, no. You have me surrounded, croakers."

The bullfrogs paused, until a tree frog from above peeped, "Take him down!"

Four tree-frog tongues shot down from the branches, and the three bullfrogs charged, ribbeting war cries. Marmoo just stood there, his pincers raised, and let the frogs whack at him. They wore themselves out quickly, barely managing to scratch the scorpion lord's new carapace. Finally, tired of playing games, Marmoo stung a bullfrog, then dragged the tree frogs from the branches and smashed them across the clearing.

Pigo heard his fellow scorpions cheer as Marmoo gave a bellow and pounded two more bullfrogs into the ground. "You should pray for the Kulipari to come— so you can watch me kill them instead of you. Here, I'll send them smoke signals."

His lorship grabbed a pincerful of embers from the campfire and scattered them on a pile of dried leaves.

When the flames caught, Marmoo started to rampage. He tore through every platypus and frog brave enough to face him, slashing and snapping and stabbing. He seemed to thrum with power as he darted to the riverbank in a frenzy of destruction. He clawed deep into the platypus burrows, tearing the contents to pieces before ripping the overhanging roots from the trees.

He paused only when Pigo arrived over the bridge made from a fallen tree.

"Round up the platypuses," Marmoo commanded. "Don't let even a single pup get away."

30

RANCHES SLAPPED DAREL'S FACE AS he raced through the woods, heading toward the river. They needed to talk to the Stargazer. They needed to save the platypus village.

He bounded forward, his toe pads aching and twigs scratching his side. From close behind, Gee called directions—he was the only one who knew the way to the platypus village. Quoba was ahead of them, moving through the trees like a fish through water . . . but she had an unfair advantage.

She'd tapped her poison.

Only a little, so far. She was barely glowing. Still, Darel felt a twinge of worry. Yabber told him that Quoba shouldn't risk tapping her poison again, because if she pushed herself, she might burn out. She'd grow weak and pale, and lose her powers forever.

"Quoba," he called, keeping his voice low.

She kept leaping through the woods ahead.

"Quoba!" he croaked again, a little louder.

This time she stopped, and a moment later he landed beside her. "Are you sure you should be tapping into—"

"Shh!" she said, raising a toe pad. "Can you smell something?"

He sniffed. "Is that smoke?"

"We're too late," she said as Gee landed beside them, panting heavily. "He set the village on fire."

"We need a plan," Darel said, swallowing his nervousness. "We need to—"

"—save them," Gee finished, and he exploded forward, moving faster than Darel had ever seen before.

"That works," Quoba said, and she sprang after Gee.

Darel leaped closer to the village. The day seemed to darken as smoke blew toward him. He blinked his inner eyelids and hopped to the top of a fallen log. Screams sounded through the haze and ash, followed by the crashing of frenzied destruction.

Flames licked at the underbrush. Darel squared his shoulders, drew his dagger, and crept through the smoke until he came to the edge of a clearing. The charred remains of a party were scattered across the forest floor, and moaning platypuses and wounded bullfrogs lay in heaps. Scorp soldiers prowled in circles around dozens of platypups, keeping them penned in.

In other circumstances, Darel might've grinned at the bizarre-looking platypuses, but at the moment they just looked terrified. Oh! And there was Chief Olba, hidden among them, standing with Coorah and Old Jir and some tree frogs.

No sign of Gee, though.

Or of Marmoo.

As Darel scanned for them, Quoba tapped into her full poison, and with a sudden blaze of color, she launched herself into the thick of the scorpions, her staff raised overhead.

The scorps spun toward her, and her staff started cracking skulls. The scorps staggered, swiping at her with poison-dripping tails, but in a flash three of them lay in a heap on the ground. Two others attacked— and missed. Quoba dodged and leaped, and slammed another in the head, knocking it unconscious. The remaining scorps charged her in an icy, disciplined silence, a squad of elite red-banded scorps.

And Darel saw two things at once: He saw Gee leading the platypuses to safety, with Coorah and Arabanoo helping the platypups keep up. And he saw an opening. He couldn't beat red-banded scorpions head on, so he'd attack them from the rear.

When a scorpion pivoted toward Quoba, Darel leaped at it from behind. In midair, he shot his tongue at a low-hanging branch, then *sucked* himself closer, supercharging his leap with the tugging of his tongue.

His dagger glinted with all the colors of the rainbow before he plunged it hilt-deep in carapace. The scorp shrieked and fled through the smoke and rubble—but another scorpion lunged at Darel, ramming him so hard that he swung up and over the tree branch, still attached by his tongue. He zoomed in a fast circle, then kicked the scorpion in the face with all his might. The scorp staggered, snapping the air with its pincers, and collapsed.

"Ha!" Darel cried, in victory.

He sucked his tongue into his mouth and landed on his toe pads, pretty pleased with himself.

Without warning, a scorpion slammed into him from behind. Pain burst in his back and he felt breathless and faint. The scorpion's tail blurred through the air at Darel's neck. He desperately parried with the dagger, but he was too dazed, too slow.

And . . . *thunk!*

31

THE SCORPION'S STINGER SANK into Quoba's staff, which she'd thrust in front of Darel at the last second.

She was glowing so brightly that Darel's eyes watered. *Too brightly.* She was tapping the last of her poison as she spun her staff, whipping the scorpion into a charred tree trunk. Then the ground. Then the mound of scorp warriors she'd already beaten. Then the ground again.

Finally, she hurled the limp warrior into the river, where it slammed a bunch of scorpions and spiders off the log bridge they'd built. The bridge groaned, swayed—then splintered. Dozens of logs splashed into the river, trapping all the remaining scorpions on the far bank.

"Thanks," Darel said.

"No problem." Quoba coughed weakly. "Well, one problem."

"What's that?"

"I've got nothing left." Her glow faded, and she swayed. "I . . . I can barely stand."

"Don't worry about *that*," Marmoo sneered, scuttling into the clearing. "I'd just knock you down anyway."

Darel slitted his nostrils in fear. They were facing Lord Marmoo alone, and Quoba was about to pass out.

The scorpion lord lashed with his tail at a moss-covered boulder as he scuttled closer. His stinger gouged a divot in the rock, spraying sharp stone chips in every direction. Oh, boy. Marmoo wasn't just bigger than before; he'd basically turned into the scorpion version of a Kulipari.

And the real Kulipari couldn't stop him.

Darel glanced toward Quoba, and almost whimpered when he saw her skin paling.

"I've got . . . enough poison," she told Marmoo, gasping for breath. "To handle . . . *you*."

But if she tapped any more poison, she'd turn white and frail, and never fight again. And for what? For nothing. Because Marmoo would still destroy them all.

No. Darel couldn't let that happen. Maybe he wasn't a real Kulipari, but he'd stop Marmoo somehow. He bulged his eyes, checking the clearing. At least the platypuses were gone. Gee and Coorah had led them away. But Marmoo could still catch them—unless Darel held him off.

"I was hoping to wipe out *all* of the Kulipari today." Marmoo snapped a pincer for emphasis. "Then lead my horde through the tear in the Veil without anyone to stop me. No matter—after I finish you, I'll track down your little friends . . ."

"Get out of here," Darel murmured to Quoba as the scorpion lord continued to gloat. "I'll keep Marmoo busy."

"He's too strong," Quoba whispered back.

"He's strong, but I'm fast. At least I can distract him until the platypuses are safe."

"You can't—"

"Go!" Darel pushed himself to his feet. "Hey, Marmoo! Remember me?"

The scorpion's side eyes flickered toward him. Then his pincers clenched, and hatred gleamed in his main eyes. "You! You're the croaker called Darel."

"That's right." Darel tensed, every muscle taut.

"How's your underbelly feeling?" He'd stabbed Marmoo's soft underside the last time they'd fought.

"Invulnerable." Marmoo's mouthparts moved into a smirk. "How are your legs?"

"My legs? They're fine."

"Yes," Marmoo said, creeping toward him, "and they'll be delicious in barbecue sauce."

Darel edged sideways, away from Quoba, suppressing a shiver of fear as Marmoo loomed through the smoky air. The scorpion lord's segmented legs picked over the charred ground and his pincers slowly opened, each one big enough to slice a bullfrog in two.

Darel gulped. He wanted to run. He wanted to leap away as fast as he could.

Instead, he gripped his dagger tight and waited. He needed to give everyone time to flee. From the corner of his eye, he caught a glimpse of Quoba hobbling into the woods, barely able to move. He didn't look closer, because he wanted to keep the scorpion lord focused on him. But he couldn't let Marmoo get too near. If Marmoo got too near, he was dead.

He raised his dagger. "First you have to catch me, *Wormoo*."

"That won't be a problem," Marmoo said, and he lunged forward, swiping at Darel with a pincer.

As Darel sprang away, he immediately knew that he was too slow. Way too slow. This new Marmoo moved as fast as Dingo.

The pincer slammed into Darel's chest with the force of a boulder and batted him across the clearing. He landed in a patch of pebbles and scraped across the ground toward the riverbank. This new Marmoo was as strong as Ponto, too.

32

DAREL PUSHED HIMSELF TO HIS knees at the top of the riverbank. Pain throbbed in his ribs and burned along his side. He wiped dirt from his face and blinked a few times, trying to clear his vision.

A black shape blurred into view, and he saw Marmoo skittering closer, an evil grin on his mouthparts.

Darel summoned all his strength, rose to his feet—and fell backward. He tumbled down the muddy bank, past roots and stones, and smacked into the hard-packed mud beside the river.

His ears rang. He saw stars—flashing, blinking stars and squiggles. Fuzzy, colorful lines, and curves in the sudden mist that rose from the river and surrounded him.

"Blue Sky King," a soft voice murmured.

Darel blinked at the old, gray-furred platypus who appeared beside him. "Who—who are you?"

"I am the Stargazer," she said, and she seemed to waver in the mist.

Darel couldn't tell if she was real or a mirage, but he said, "I need help. *We* need help. Marmoo's about to—"

"I cannot fight him," the Stargazer said in her gentle voice. "I'm too deep in a trance, but I have a message for you, from the Rainbow Serpent."

For a moment, Darel forgot his pain and fear. He forgot that Marmoo was clattering toward the top of the riverbank to finish him off.

"I—I—I saw the Serpent, rising from a mountain spring," he said. "It spoke to me."

"The Serpent spoke to your father, too, and showed him visions of the future, which he drew in the Snowy Mountain caves. He didn't understand the visions, but they weren't for him. They were for you."

"F-f-for me?"

"You aren't a Kulipari, Darel. But you are so much more."

She glanced at the river, and when Darel followed her gaze, his breath caught. A brilliant misty arc curved over the water, the colors rippling and glowing in the current.

"Think back," the Stargazer told him. "Remember

the paintings. *You* understand. Your father's drawings are speaking to you. You know what you must do."

"I don't know anything! And Marmoo's about to *eat* me!"

"Remember the painting. The rainbow, seeping underground..."

"But what does that mean? I remember the stencils, the frogs and scorps, the tadpole with the pointy tail. Burnu said it was a boomerang."

"Not a tail, Blue Sky King. Not a boomerang. A dagger."

And in that moment, Darel *did* know. He knew why the Rainbow Serpent had sent those visions to his father. He knew why the rainbow had plunged underground. He knew why his father's dagger had shone so brilliantly on the mountaintop. And he knew why the Serpent had told the platypuses to dig tunnels and underground pools.

The colors shining in the river grew brighter and brighter. Darel caught his breath, listening to the rainbow, which splashed and gurgled in a voice like the Rainbow Serpent.

Then the mist cleared, and the Stargazer was gone. He was alone.

Well, except for Marmoo, pacing atop the river-bank.

Darel pushed himself to his knees. He ached all over, but he made himself ignore the pain. He wasn't going down without a fight—especially not now that he'd finally figured out what the Rainbow Serpent wanted from him.

Slitting his nostrils in determination, he leaped to the top of the riverbank . . . but when he landed, he wobbled, barely able to stay upright.

And Lord Marmoo loomed over him, just a few feet away.

"Not much of a fighter, are you?" Marmoo sneered. "At least the Kulipari will give me a workout."

"I'm not done yet," Darel groaned, pulling out his dagger.

In a flash, Marmoo's pincer smashed him in the chest again. Darel scraped across the ground and ended in a tangled, painful heap. He couldn't fight. He couldn't stand. He could barely breathe.

"Any last words?" Marmoo asked, his stinger curving close.

33

I HAVE SOMETHING TO SAY," A VOICE murmured from across the clearing.

Marmoo cocked his head, and Darel glanced aside . . . then gaped in shock when he saw a stocky black-skinned frog with a red dot on her forehead. Chief Olba. She was completely alone, and completely unarmed, except for a *quandong* in one hand, a shiny red fruit like a peach.

"Chief!" he croaked. *"Run!"*

She shook her head and hopped closer to Marmoo. "I'm here to talk to the scorpion lord," she said. "Leader to leader."

Darel opened his mouth to shout *"He'll kill you! Run! You can't fight Marmoo with a peach!"* But Marmoo kicked him in the stomach with one of his middle legs.

"So you're Olba." Marmoo's mouthparts moved into a cold smile. "Never thought I'd see you this far from the Veil."

"Oh, I'm a big fan of sightseeing." Chief Olba opened her mouth to bite the juicy quandong, and

Darel moaned. How could she think of food at a time like this? She was worse than Gee. But she lowered the fruit before eating it and continued, "And I heard you were threatening the platypus tribe."

Marmoo snapped a pincer. "I'll kill them all."

"Why?"

"Why not?"

"Surely you have a better reason than that."

"They follow the Rainbow Serpent." Marmoo sidled closer to her. "Killing them will draw the Kulipari here. And they look tasty."

"Three reasons!" Olba nodded. "I'm impressed."

"I know what you're doing, Olba."

She sniffed the quandong. "What am I doing?"

"Trying to delay me, so the swamp rats get away." He snapped a pincer near the chief's head. "But I'll catch them easily, even after ripping you and the wood frog into pieces. I'm faster than you can imagine."

Darel took a shaky breath and pushed himself into a crouch. The world tilted, and he felt a trickle of blood running down one leg. Still, he needed to save the chief. He needed to distract Marmoo.

"Hey, lizard-lungs," he croaked, raising his dagger.

In a blur, Marmoo grabbed Darel's throat with a pincer. "I just can't decide which of you to kill first."

"Urk!" Darel said, choking.

"You're not very smart, are you?" Olba asked Marmoo. "You've got the chief of the Amphibilands in your grasp, and you're wasting time with a wood frog. I suppose it's all that desert sand clogging up your brain."

She popped the quandong into her mouth and turned to hop away.

Marmoo bellowed in anger, tossed Darel aside, and sprang after her.

Darel hit the ground hard, then watched in horror as Marmoo pounced on the portly Chief Olba. All the scorpion's eyes narrowed in rage, his massive pincers clenched, and his whipcord tail blurred forward as fast as thought.

And Marmoo's stinger pierced the chief's back. A direct hit, a deathblow.

Olba stumbled, stuck on the stinger like a fish on a hook.

"Nooo!" Darel gasped. "No, no . . ."

Chief Olba turned her head and looked at Marmoo with her dying eyes . . . and she smiled.

"Are you *laughing* at me?" Marmoo snarled, bringing her close to his face with his tail. "What are you doing?"

She spat the quandong into his open mouth, the bulging skin of the fruit still shiny and unbroken—and as he chomped down, she whispered, "I'm giving you a gift. It's filled with pepperbush juice . . ."

She went limp, dangling on the end of Marmoo's tail.

As Darel crawled toward her, the fruit—hollowed out, and filled with Coorah's pepperbush goop—burst inside Marmoo's mouth. Maybe his carapace was invulnerable, but his throat was still sensitive.

The scorpion lord howled in agony and flung Olba away, shaking his head violently, trying to escape the scorching burn. He scooped pincerfuls of dirt from the ground and shoved them into his mouth. Then, roaring in pain, he crashed through the underbrush toward the river. His screaming stopped only when he reached the river, where he tried desperately to wash the goop from his mouthparts.

"Open your eyes." Darel cradled Chief Olba's head in his arms. "Open your eyes, Chief! You'll be okay. I'll get Coorah. I'll get Yabber! We'll—"

She touched his face with a toe pad. "Darel? There's . . . something you must do."

"Anything. Anything at all."

Her voice faded to a whisper. "Keep them safe."

Then she died in his arms.

The scorpion lord bellowed and raced into the clearing, desperate for relief from the burning goop—in too much pain to threaten Darel.

And that's when Darel saw them: Gee and Coorah, Quoba and Arabanoo and all the platypuses, stepping from the trees. One look at their faces told him why they'd come back. To save *him*. To fight Marmoo, even though they knew they'd lose.

For a moment, Marmoo's agonized bellows quieted as he eyed the grim faces of his enemies. Then he shook his head violently, his mouthparts still burning, blundered into the woods in the other direction, and vanished.

As his friends gathered around him, Darel sat with the chief's body in his arms, tears running down his face.

When he finally raised his head, silence fell. "I know what to do," he said, his voice somber. "I know how to end the fighting, once and for all."

"How?" Gee asked.

"We start," Darel told him, "by tearing down the Veil."

ABOUT THE AUTHORS AND ILLUSTRATOR

TREVOR PRYCE is a retired NFL player and writer who's written for the *New York Times* and NBC.com. He's also developed television and movie scripts for Sony Pictures, Cartoon Network, Disney, ABC, and HBO, among others. He lives in Maryland.

JOEL NAFTALI is the author of many books, several written with his wife, Lee. He lives in California.

SANFORD GREENE is an accomplished comics illustrator whose work has been published by Marvel, DC Comics, Disney, Nickelodeon, Dark Horse, and more. He lives in South Carolina.